27011
WELCOME TO WHITLOCK 2.3

A. A. DARK

Mad Girl
PUBLISHING

International Bestselling Author
A.A. Dark
Copyright © 2018 by Mad Girl Publishing

All Rights Reserved

PROLOGUE

BRAM

To understand oneself, you had to be truthful about who you were. It was no secret I wasn't a good man. If I wanted to be honest about who Bram Whitlock *truly* was, I had to look deep within and peel back the layers of desensitized evil I had become accustomed to.

From my earliest days, I had been exposed to torture—to rape and death of the vilest nature. *Monsters.* It was such a widely used term to describe men like me. Men who could stare you in the eyes while they took away your very existence. Men who got pleasure in doing so. But what was it to kill others just as corrupt and malicious as yourself? Did it matter? Was it redeeming in any way?

Perhaps it was debatable. It was nothing, *yet everything.* But I wasn't just a killer. I was a ruler of an underground fortress housing sex slaves. And I allowed for the continuation. I always would—until my dying breath. Why? The answer was simple. If I didn't, someone else would. At least I could control the age of the slaves. I could monitor the horrors in my home. It wasn't moral, but neither was life. Being the Main Master of such a place didn't allow for leniency or feelings. That got you murdered, making you irrelevant in the grander scheme of things. Not long ago, my best friend had almost succeeded in taking my life. When he failed and showed me the horrors this place could truly become, I came back with a vengeance to set things right. One so powerful, it cost me not only most of my board members, but the respect of the only person I loved: *Everleigh,* slave *twenty-four-six-ninety.*

Monster. Yes, I was that. With my numb emotions came our distance to one another. Instead of being there for her and trying to help the broken woman she had become because of West Harper, my focus was on revenge. Weeks of rage left me blinded to the signs before me. I lost her. And not just her trust or love, but she escaped Whitlock. *She escaped me.*

And so, the cycle of my obsession reignited. The deadness within melted like acid at the news of her escape, and my sins... they were reborn.

Regret was something I rarely felt. With Everleigh, I was drowning in it. All I had were what-ifs. They sung the most grievous mantra of mourning. Awake. Asleep. The nightmares that developed concerning her safety and distance plagued my soul like nothing ever had.

I.

Love.

You.

I.

Love.

You.

God, I loved her. For hours, I had texted those words to my slave. Even as my fingers got tired from the constant typing, there was no way I could stop trying to show her the fervor of my infatuation. Months of desperate intensity at her missing presence soared to heights I could barely contain within my aching chest. I had to do everything in my power to make her see the truth. She had to know why I couldn't set her free. It wasn't just because of the Whitlock laws binding her to my fortress. I couldn't release her...*for myself.*

Love. *Obsessive love.* It had always been there for her. Even after my attempted murder when the trauma had taken my emotions, my brain still held to the fact that she was mine. *She'd always be mine.*

Panic—mania.

Each day was spent scouring reports on her possible whereabouts. Each second, my mind clung to her memory as if I were terrified I would never get to make more with her. *Love. Love. Love.* My heart and brain screamed at me to make this right. To find her at any cost.

And found her, I had.

Master Gavin Draper's tip brought happiness. The damaged thing in my chest had skipped in celebration. I would have her again. But it didn't last. It exploded in agony when we finally came face to face.

Drugged and nearly unresponsive in her guard's arms, she lay there helpless because of me. I thought by having Master Draper drug her, it would allow Everleigh to remain calm as I explained my feelings for her. I could prepare her for our return to Whitlock and the way things had to be. I knew she wouldn't like what I had in store, but she didn't have a choice. *Neither did I.*

None of it mattered. The plan went up in flames right there over Everleigh's shoulder and arm from a blowtorch. My slave's guard used her hostage against me. He hurt her, keeping enough distance and leverage to have me spinning in circles of fury. She was gone. Again. And injured, because she couldn't fight against what the guard thought was best. The pain she must have been in was all my fault, but I wouldn't back off. I couldn't.

I always seemed to hurt her in one way or another. A real man would have set her free. A real man would have accepted the loss and known she would have been happier without coming

back to the black hole of Whitlock. I wasn't a real man; I was a
monster of men. One who knew how neurotically far gone he
was and didn't give a shit. I had said it a million times. Even as I
stared across my jet at Everleigh's new slave, Eleven, my brain
chanted the truth in repetition of a single word: *mine*.

AAMIR

*P*araלyzed. Even drugged and unable to move, I couldn't fight the effects of the mourning engulfing every inch of my insides. Tears ran down the sides of my face, and every so often, a sound managed to claw its way free from my throat. My twin was gone. No...*I was gone from her.* Taken by the Main Master who silently sat on his expensive leather chair inside the jet we were on. Layla and I had never been apart for more than a few hours. Not once in our entire lives. And now, we were. Possibly forever, if the bastard had his way.

Layla. She was all I could think about. All I could see as I relived the horrible nightmare of the guards opening the cell in Master Draper's dungeon and tearing us away from each other. They said we were slaves. I was meant to be sold at Whitlock, while she'd stay at Red Island with Master Draper because of her accident and the scar running down her forehead. As if she wasn't good enough for where I was going. As if...

This wasn't happening.

A deep, broken-up sob left my lips as my chest shook from the cries that couldn't be contained. I had promised to protect her. I had sworn to her I'd keep her safe. I hadn't. Not just from

Ram, the giant on the ship that had transported us, but myself. Layla was right. I should have killed both of us before allowing Ram to manipulate me into raping her. I had convinced myself I had fucked my own sister to save her life. But had I? Had I really helped her by prolonging the horrors she now faced with the Dragon? What if Master Draper...

More sounds left me as thoughts collided among a million others. More tears.

"Jesus. Enough. I get it, slave. You wanted her to come. Everleigh gave you hope and I'm the bad guy for taking it away."

Main Master Whitlock stood as he glared down at me with blue eyes—heartless, enraged eyes. It was sheer luck I was paralyzed facing his way or I wouldn't have been able to see the multiple expressions that crossed his face as he began to pace and steal glances my way.

"Whitlock is not a charity house. It's a hellhole. Get that through your thick head. Have you learned nothing so far? This life you now live will not get better. It will get worse. And for reasons you have no business knowing, I refused to sell you two together. You should have never been taken as a pair to begin with. Yes, I could have sold Nine, but you would have liked that outcome a lot worse. Did you want your sister to become food for the scavengers? *Dead?* That's what would have happened in her condition. You think you've lost her because you can't see her? Because she's not close? Would it have made you feel better to have her next door so you could endure her screams? *No.* Now you will never know whether she's dead or alive, and that, slave, is a fucking *blessing* in this world."

He growled at my near-silent cries. Turning, he ate up the space as his fingers pushed through his dark hair. Moments passed before he pulled out a phone, only to shove it back in his pocket, a collection of emotions sweeping over his nearly perfect features.

"Everleigh. Jesus, what are you doing? What do you want with a male slave? I know *why*, but what are your true motives in this game you're playing?" A hard stare moved over me as the Main Master came forward. "In-house protector? You're built. You're a fighter, or you were. It didn't take me five minutes to discover your life story. If I know, she would know...but I'd fucking protect her. Unless..." He gave a hard shake, as if he didn't like where his thoughts were going. "She fears me. She *should* fucking fear me. But..." Again, he stopped as he continued walking back and forth, seeming to forget about me. "*I love her*. I made a mistake once in the White Room. I wouldn't do that again. She has to know I wasn't myself."

Tingling drew me even farther from his mindless whispers as I managed to wiggle my toe. Even with all my strength, it would barely move. A groan had him looking back in my direction.

"Wearing off, I see. It doesn't matter. We'll be at Whitlock before you can so much as speak."

"W-Wr...ong."

The word had come from nowhere, and yet, every part of me. The Main Master raised one of his eyebrows and twisted his mouth.

"So it would seem, but you know what?" Challenging eyes narrowed as he reached the counter and lifted a vile. "I'm only wrong for as long as it takes to be right. I always have a backup plan. Never forget that. Never underestimate me, Eleven. Who you see is exactly the person I want you to. What you hear, I want you to hear. The way you live or die...*me*. It's all up to me, slave. I am your God, your devil. Your religion and survival. I am the one and only thing that allows your world to go round." My finger moved, and he smiled. "I have to give Everleigh that much. She's opened my eyes and made me step up my game."

My breaths grew heavier as I tried to make more words come.

"You still have a good hour before you're back to normal.

7

Before then, you and I will part ways. It doesn't change the fact that you're going to help me. Funny thing is, you don't even know it. We're going to share something special, Eleven. Just wait and see. Everleigh thinks she's in control. Little does she know, the game she plays belongs to me as well."

"ETA: fifteen minutes."

A blurry silhouette disappeared just as fast as it had popped the top half of its body in behind Master Whitlock. He didn't say a word as he came closer.

"Do you love her? The brunette in the bedroom? Jessa, I believe you said, earlier. She's yours, is she not?"

I tried to get my voice to work again, but it wouldn't.

"What bad luck you have being brought to me. Your sister, your love—those closest to you have been thrust into my world to be used and die. I almost feel sorry for you. Perhaps, this is what my slave feels."

Puzzlement clouded his face as he slowly walked over and took a seat. The minutes stretched, and I somehow cleared my throat before forcing the one word out.

"Any-thing."

The Main Master glanced over.

"I already have everything."

My grunt drew his attention, and my desperation grew the closer we got to landing. I may never get an opportunity to see him again.

"Not...the Mis-tress. Not her."

Dark hair swayed against the sides of his face as he snapped his focus on me. "Watch it, Eleven. What I need you for doesn't permit you to be able to talk."

"Let..." seconds followed, "...me. I'll bring her here. I'll... my sister."

A smirk pulled at his full lips as he crossed his arms over his chest and looked ahead. Silence. I could feel us dropping in altitude. Panic had my leg moving up along the sofa I laid on. I wasn't bound. There had been no need once the drug kicked in. It was as if the Main Master wasn't worried about what I was capable of in the least.

"Anything," I breathed out. "My...*sister.*"

Moments passed. Torturous, long seconds.

"Do you know what they call birds that have been set free from their cages, slave?" Confusion blanked my mind as Master Whitlock once again turned his blue eyes on me. "Dinner. Not free. They are food for the foul. You see, once set loose, it doesn't understand the rules of the real world. It has been trained to its conditions, broken within its mind, therefore losing sight the moment it gains freedom. If released from her cage, your sister will perish and surely crumble to reality. She has endured the worst of men. In her mind, all she knows at this point is to survive. To fight. If you take that away from her, she has nothing left. There is no coming back from what she's been through. Surely you know that."

"I...*need her.*"

Tears came again. My fingers slowly drew into a fist, and I managed to rotate my head the smallest amount. A steady pounding plagued my temples, but I didn't care.

"You don't. And she doesn't need you. I wasn't going to tell you this, but what the hell. It's not like you're going anywhere. Maybe it'll help ease the guilt over your...*guilt.*" He took a deep breath. "Master Draper told me he will keep her in the tower adjoining his bedroom, housing the most luxurious amenities. She will be dressed in silk and pampered. She is a slave of status now, given she belongs to the Main Master. There's nothing to worry about. Cherish the thought. Reality for her here would be far less grand. She'd be lucky to last a month. Master Draper will take good care of her unless she gives him reason not to."

Was that supposed to make me feel better? My anxiety heightened. I knew my twin. I knew her pride and fearlessness. Material possessions or status meant nothing to her. She would give him a million reasons to kill her, and he eventually would. With us separated and no help in sight, she had no reason to live. If she didn't kill herself, the Dragon would end her life. It was only a matter of time.

The jolt from the plane landing jumpstarted my heart. The hard thumping in my chest left me weaker. My fingers unfurled from my fist and my eyes rolled for the briefest second. A fog took over my mind, and before I knew it, the Main Master was standing and looking down at me. Opening the vial, he used the dabber to rub oil over my forehead, almost seeming to spell something out.

"This is where we say goodbye until auction night."

With that, the tall man I'd grown to hate in such a brief time disappeared. Footsteps stomped passed, and Jessa was carried from the room. Before I could attempt to yell for them to put her down, another man easily lifted me and threw me over his shoulder. Dead weight and gravity pulled at my limp arms as they swung and bounced uselessly against the man's wide back. My eyes rolled, and just like my life, time was stolen from me once again.

SCOUT 19

"*L*ook at me! Just…*look at me*! I look like a fool. Like a goddamn fucking idiot. I'm gonna kill her. I swear, when she gets found, I'm going to…"

Master Barclane's face was bright red as he paced in front of the large television covering his living room wall. Most didn't care for the luxuries of television amid their private sadistic spaces, but Master Barclane was a rarity. He more lived in Whitlock than being the occasional Master who only appeared when they were ready to commit their evil deeds. Unfortunately for him, he'd gone to his private residence in Cheyenne only hours ago and had been bombarded by the press.

"Do you see how I'm caught unaware? Look at the shock on my face as they practically shove the microphone down my throat. Everleigh! That bitch. I know she was behind it. She probably blames *me* for Bram almost catching her. I wish he would have. I wish—" A strangled sound left him as his fist waved at the television. A soft giggle had me glancing toward a blonde standing in the bedroom door. The smile melted from her face as she quickly disappeared back behind the wall.

"Calm, Master. It doesn't have to be a bad thing. It's not

11

every day one gets nominated for a Child Abuse Intervention Award in the outside world."

"That award is going to eat me alive if..." His eyes cut away from me, returning to the news program he had recorded. "I can't believe she donated all those millions in my name, making it look as if it came from me. Me! That...fucking...*cunt!* It's a warning. The Main Master has her slave and gave another away to Master Draper. I heard all about it. She's pissed that her plans got foiled and she's taking it out on me. She's—fuck!"

Again, his hand sliced through the air.

"Master Barclane, are you sure Mistress Harper is the one who did this? It's only been a little over twenty-four hours from when she was almost caught. Rumor has it she was injured, and badly."

A loud growl tore through the room. "You know nothing! Everleigh could be on death's doorstep and wouldn't go down without fucking everyone else with her last breath. The woman is all revenge and twice as evil. She is behind this. I know she is, and so help me, you're going to find her and make her pay. You're going to—" Barclane glanced toward the ceiling in the corner of the room and lowered his voice as he stepped in closer, using me as a shield to the camera we both knew was recording our every move. "Kill her. I want that bitch dead before the Main Master has a chance to find her. Alive, she's a threat to us all."

"Do you realize what you're asking of me? If the Main Master knew why you called me here, and I went along with this, we'd both be dead."

There was a pause as the Master studied my face. "You should be one of us. I know that as well as everyone else. I can do that for you. I can make it worth your while."

"Is that so?"

More hesitation. "Ten million dollars. Half now, half when she's dead."

My lips pressed together as I pushed away temptation. Ten

million was a lot of money—more than I had earned so far being a scout. But my status…

"Thank you for the offer, but I'll have to give it consideration."

"I don't have time to wait around for your answer. You have until midnight."

"And if I say no?"

The Master crossed his arms over his chest as he went back to gazing at the television. "You would be wise not to. Accidents happen at Shady Falls Retirement Home all the time."

A laugh left me. Not from shock or even as a mask to cover the fear of my mother's wellbeing. The sound was heartless, just like me. "You think I care if you kill that bitch? You must not have dug as deep as you should have. That woman turned her back on me for drugs over thirteen years ago. She's been dead to me since. She's a fucking vegetable. End her so-called life if you wish, but it will not sway my decision."

I left without another word. The surge into the hallway had cold air slamming into my lungs. It got trapped in my chest as I collided with a passing slave. She bounced to the side, crashing into the wall and lowering her head as she caught herself and took off in a jog.

This wasn't the first time I was asked to do something behind the Main Master's back. Plenty of times Masters had searched me out because of my bloodline. But this wasn't scouting. This wasn't taking a hand-picked innocent off the streets to be introduced to Whitlock. *No.* This was killing my Main Master's slave. This was treason in the most corrupt form.

Repeatedly, I clenched my jaw as I headed through the maze of white. A hall this way. One that way. Turning and twisting led me deeper within the fortress while I let the offer sink in. There was a lot I could do with that money, but what was status or cash if I got caught? Bram would kill me. Or worse…Everleigh would. It wasn't like she was alone. She had men guarding her.

How many, there was no telling. And the amount protecting her mattered. Who was I to accomplish something no one else had? I wasn't stupid. I didn't think I was smarter or stronger than the highly trained men already searching. If I went, I would more than likely die. Then where would ten million get me?

I found myself slowing at the turn leading to the Main Master's wing. Should I tell him of this betrayal? Should I—

"Nineteen. Kinda far from Scout Quarters. Bored like me?"

I glanced behind, seeing a fellow scout approach. The weight at my hip registered, but I smiled, even as I stayed on-guard. Trust was for fools at Whitlock. I had learned that in my earliest days.

"You could say that. What are you doing here? I thought you were in New York."

"I was. Just came in to check with Boss to see how things were going with the search." Fourteen paused and glanced over his shoulder. "I'm not going to lie; I saw you leaving Master Barclane's."

"And?"

Dark eyes narrowed the smallest amount before he threw me a fake smile. "Nothing. Say, you didn't happen to catch a glimpse of his slave in there, did you? Blonde. Tall. Beautiful."

"I saw her."

I started walking as he followed. There was something suspicious as his features tightened in thought.

"How was she? I found her, by the way."

"Did you? Congrats on that. I'm sure she made you a lot of money."

"Yeah, it's whatever. How did she look? Was she doing okay? I mean…"

Glancing over, I slowed as he threw me an angry look.

"What? I can't ask how she is?"

"I didn't say anything."

"You didn't have to. I see the way you're looking at me. I'll be blunt. *Charlee is mine.* Master Barclane may own her, but I'll do with her as I please. I want to see her. I want you to help me."

"You've lost your fucking mind. If you were caught, he'd kill you for touching what's his."

"She's mine, or did you miss that part?"

A silent laugh left me. "You fell for a slave. *Unbelievable.* You, of all people. Do you really think she'd see you after you brought her here? After you ruined her life? If you go to her, she'll tell him. She'll tell her Master, and you'll be as good as dead."

"Charlee wouldn't do that. I'm the only hope she has for believing she can escape this place. She'll try to play me, and I'll let her...so long as I get what I want."

"Have I already said unbelievable? You're as fucked-up as they come. I'm not helping you."

"Then let me ask you this. What did he want? A new slave? A secret kidnapping? Would our Main Master approve?"

My feet planted, and before I could stop myself, I had Fourteen's shirt fisted in my palm as I slammed him against the wall. "Don't threaten me. I'm not the one trying to fuck a Master's slave. Stay away. If you come near me again, I *will* inform Master Barclane, and we both know what will happen then."

I pushed my fist into his chest, then let go of his shirt before stalking back the way I came. The morning had been too much. No one pushed me around. No one gave me orders I wasn't okay with. Only one man ran this place, and it was about time he and I had a talk.

"Where are you going? Nineteen!"

The glare I threw had the scout growing quiet. I took a right, heading toward my Main Master's wing. Guards thickened at every turn. Some nodded, while others eyed me uncertainly. It wasn't common for scouts to go straight to Bram Whitlock. We went to Mateo, the scout leader, our boss. Not this time. Not for the news I had to share.

The incline in the hall gradually rose and I took a left, bringing me a good twenty feet from his door. Two guards were standing ahead—one on each side.

"Has he returned?"

My question had them standing straighter. "He has, but you're not on the list. Did you have an appointment?"

"No. He won't care that I'm here. I think he'll want to see me."

There was no response as I stopped short of them. One pulled out a phone.

"Number?"

"Scout Nineteen."

He dialed, bringing the phone to his ear. "Sorry to bother you, Main Master, but a scout is here. Says he needs to talk to you." The tall man's mouth closed. As he reopened it to speak, the door swung open. The anger on the Main Master's face had us all frozen at his glare.

"This better be good."

The door opened wider, and I took a deep breath before heading into the large apartment. A little dark-haired boy was rolling a ball across the floor to an older woman in the living area, and the smell of food lingered.

"My office."

The command had me following down a hall to the first door on the right. Books lined the shelves, covering the entire back wall, and a large desk sat centered before them. Master Whitlock leaned against the desk and cocked his head, waiting for me to begin.

"May I?"

He nodded as I gripped the doorknob. I shut it, swallowing hard. He didn't fear me, and it showed. The knife he kept under his suit jacket never left him. It was common knowledge, and I wouldn't have to get close for him to kill me with it.

"Are you here to offer to catch my slave too?"

"Uh...no, Main Master."

"I haven't been home but a few hours and two scouts have already come to me. If you're not here about my slave, then what is it?"

One step. Two. I got closer, letting out a deep breath. "I am actually here about your slave, but not because I want to capture her. I've been made an offer."

"An offer? An offer for what?"

The interest was there, piqued, as he reached down to grip the edge of the desk with one hand. Whiter, his fingers became as he waited.

"I've been offered ten million dollars to kill her."

Silence.

Blue eyes darkened as he slowly rose from the desk. "Kill her? And who made this offer?"

My mouth opened. "...Master Barclane, sir. Not fifteen minutes ago. He invited me to his apartment where he asked. He believes she's behind the award he received. A child abuse award because of a donation. It angered him. He thinks she's a risk not only to him, but Whitlock.

"Is that right? And what did you tell him? Does he know you're here?"

My head shook. "No, Main Master. I told him I needed time to think over his offer. I have until midnight."

"I see." Bram headed for the small bar, pouring a scotch and finishing it in one drink as he kept his back to me. Time seemed to stretch forever.

"At ten-till, you'll knock on his door. You will accept his offer. You will tell him you've already discussed your need to join the search and Mateo will be giving you an answer soon. Then, you will head to the Cradle where I will have your orders and assignment waiting." He turned, setting down the glass. "I expect you to follow my orders to a *T*. You may not understand them, or even like them. It doesn't change the fact

17

that this is what your Main Master expects of you. Is that clear?"

"Yes, sir."

"Good. What I'm asking of you will not be an easy task. You could very well die. For that, I'll triple what Master Barclane offered, along with your rightful title if you so choose to take it. If not, you can pull guard at my side for your loyalty. Now, leave."

BRAM

*D*esperation was the downfall of all men. Master Barclane knew better than to betray me. For hours, he had watched me kill the members closest to him. Yet, when his secrets were put to the test, he went into a panic, ignoring his allegiance to the one person who held his life in the palm of their hands. He reacted, and it was in the wrong way. The death threat may have been to Everleigh, but she was mine, and he knew that.

After his call informing me of her arrival at his apartment, I knew his loyalty had to be tested. I had to know where he stood concerning my slave. After all, someday she would return. With him on the board, and her at my side, he wouldn't overlook her blackmail. He'd never trust her. For that, I needed to make sure I could trust *him* when he assumed she was at her worst.

He failed. And in more ways than one. It wasn't Everleigh who donated in his name, it was me. Had he brought his concerns to me, I would have told him I was responsible.

Taking my phone from my pocket, I bit my bottom lip and hit the button for the millionth time since I had landed. Ringing met me as I brought it to my ear, and the voicemail shortly followed.

"I have to know you're okay." My breath caught at the

turmoil twisting my gut. "It's my fault. I'm sorry. I love you, slave. You have to call me."

A squeal of laughter broke through my private barrier, and I couldn't stop my eyes from rising to the cracked door. Alvin was happy at my return. He'd rushed into my arms the moment I walked through the door and spent a good five minutes holding my leg as I'd checked the news my second-in-command had left me. It was hard adjusting to the emotions the child brought out in me, but I couldn't deny they were there. I was getting attached. A part of me might have even loved him.

Love...

Slipping the phone back in my pocket, I headed into the living area where Alvin was molded around a ball, letting it roll him off to the side. The moment he tumbled to the floor, the giggling continued. My smile was automatic, and warmth webbed in my chest.

Blue eyes lifted to mine, and he quickly got up, lifting his arms. Somewhere deep within, I knew he was too old to be held like a child. The future Master shouldn't have such coddling, but I couldn't overlook the tragedy his little mind had suffered so far. The poor child had been taken from his parents. Endured a trip all the way here with cold scouts and sobbing, hysterical slaves.

"Only for a moment." I lifted him in my arms, unable to ignore the softening at the end of my stern statement. "There's work to do. There's always lots of work."

"Play, Bram."

"I don't play. I work."

Lids narrowed, but his smile returned. "Sing to Al-vin."

"I don't sing either. I'll read to you."

The smile fell as he looked toward his room. "Ev-leigh reads. Ever-leigh."

More warmth appeared, tinted with an aching mourning. "She does. Did you like when Everleigh read to you?"

A nod was the only response he gave as he began to wiggle.

The moment I placed him down, Alvin raced for his room. Within seconds, he was back, waving his book.

"Ev-leigh. I want Ever-leigh to read."

"She can't read to you, Alvin. She's not here."

"Ever-leigh. Read to Alvin."

My head shook as I glanced at his nurse.

"He's asked about her nonstop since she left."

A curse was on the tip of my tongue, but I held it in, keeping my temper calm as the child began to yell her name and look around the room.

"Ev-leigh! Ever! Leigh!"

"Alvin."

"Ever!"

"Alvin," I said louder, nearly snatching the book. "We don't throw fits. If you throw a fit, I won't read you the book. You can play on the floor by yourself. We are leaders. You," I emphasized, "will be a leader someday. I will not have some spoiled, little...person running this place. We can't afford that. You must be reserved, but direct. If you want Everleigh, you have to make that happen. We Whitlocks do that."

A pouty lip was paired with tear-filled eyes as he watched me pull out my phone.

"Probably not the best lesson, but what the hell." I crouched, showing him the black device in my hand. "You want Everleigh?"

"Yes."

"I'm going to make a call, and you tell her. You tell her exactly what you want. That's what we do. We voice our wants. And we get what we want, Alvin. It may not be when we want it, but we don't give up, do we?"

A few seconds passed before he shook his head.

"That's right. Now, I'm going to dial this number and when I put the phone to your mouth and ear, you tell Everleigh what you want her to know."

Once again, I hit the button. Ringing sounded, and just like before: voicemail. I sighed, moving the cell to Alvin's ear. The beep was distant, but I nodded to him.

"Ever-leigh read." His lip quivered. "Ev-leigh read Alvin's book...Ever?"

The tears racing from his eyes about did me in. What had she done by coming here? She had done something to this child in minutes that me and his nurse couldn't.

"Jesus," I whispered, pulling back the phone and bringing it to my mouth as I stood. "Do you hear him? *You did this.* You better call. If not for me, at least talk to him." A wale burst through the room and my teeth ground as I angrily hung up the phone. "No. You did great. She'll call. *She better call,*" I mumbled. "Come. I'll read your book. Ms. Pat, will you make us a snack?"

"Of course, Main Master."

I barely had Alvin to my sofa before my phone had my heart exploding in rhythm. The ringing was different. It was a video call from an unknown number.

"Sit. Let's just..." I paused, "sit." Trembling took over my hand as I pressed the button. Faster, my thumping pulse left me shaking, and it all came to a crashing stop as Everleigh's pale face came into view. She was in a bed, and what looked to be half-conscious. Mascara was stained around her eyes and her hair was in a haloed mess around her head.

"Oh, God. *Everleigh.*"

"Alvin...asked for me. I want to talk to him."

"You called."

"*For him.*" A small cry left her as she shifted and blinked heavily. "You're an evil man using a child to get me to respond. For that, I'm not speaking to you yet."

"Everleigh—"

"Don't. Don't...you dare."

The slur was evident, and she yawned, only to grimace. The

22

hint of a bandage covered her shoulder. I quickly memorized everything I could about her and the luxurious, red velvet throw pillow she had to the right of her own golden pillow.

"Ever!" Alvin thrust himself in front of me, climbing onto my lap in his excitement.

"Hey, sweetie. You called me?"

"Ever-leigh read to Alvin."

"You want me to read your book? But...I don't have a copy here." Her mouth tightened as her eyes rose up to mine. "What's the book called?"

Before I could speak, Alvin held it up, pushing the cover right up against the phone. A pained laugh sounded as she repeated the title.

"Got it. I will get that book so next time I can read it to you. How...about this?"

At her break in talking, I lowered the book so I could see her again. I had to see her. To watch her lips move as that haunting voice came through.

"How about Bram reads the book this time, and you and I listen. Is that okay?"

Alvin nodded eagerly, bouncing even more in his excitement.

"Alright, *Bram*. Let's hear it."

"First, tell me how you are."

Tears trailed down her cheeks as she tried to move into more of a sitting position. A hand thrust into the camera's view, gripping just below her breasts to help lift her higher. As it did, the camera flashed to the ceiling. My growl was immediate, making Alvin jump.

"Is that him? Luke, that bast—"

"*Don't you dare say it in front of the child.* Read, Bram."

Deep breaths left me as my adrenaline soared for an entirely different reason. She came back into view, and I tried to calm myself. With one hand, I managed to open the book and start on the first sentence, but I never stopped stealing glances up.

"Engine Six is red." Quick glance up. Everleigh threw a weak smile at Alvin but lifted an eyebrow as she gave her attention to me. I looked back at the book, continuing again. "Engine six puts out fires." Easing the book to the sofa, I turned the page, lifting it awkwardly again. "Courage rides on Engine Six. He's a Dalmatian." Another glance. Everleigh was back to smiling at Alvin, but she could barely stay awake. I battled holding the phone in one hand and the book in the other. Another flip. "Courage's best friend is Phil, the firefighter. Phil is a hero."

"Wow," Everleigh said, slurring and smiling brightly. "We like heroes, don't we, Alvin?"

"Yes!"

"They're brave and strong just like you."

A squeal followed clapping, and I couldn't deny the anger over Luke's presence was fading as I soaked in my time with her and Alvin. *All of us, together.* I read in a fog, taking her in. By the time the story came to an end, I was sad. She would never be that happy toward me. Not even pretending. And I could tell she wasn't putting on a show for Alvin. She enjoyed their moment. So much so, I could see the longing. Her eyes were clouding with more tears, and I almost didn't notice Alvin climbing off my lap. So much pain in my slave—mentally, physically. And it was all because of me.

"Will you talk to me while Alvin eats his snack? Everleigh... *I'm so sorry.* I didn't think Luke would—"

"Just don't."

"I'm going into my room so we can talk privately. Private," I snapped. "I'd like that bastard who burned you to leave too."

"He's not leaving, Bram. He can't."

"What do you mean?"

I shut myself in my bedroom, pacing as I soaked in the sudden anguish lacing her drawn in features.

"He's holding the phone. I should go," she said, softly. "I can't talk right now. I..."

"*Wait.* Please, wait."

Her eyes fluttered back open, and the bright blue had me gripping the phone tighter. "I love you. I take responsibility for what's happened, and I want to make it up to you. There are reasons you're not coming home yet. I know you want to. God, slave, I feel it. You want me back. You love me too. If you return..." my brow creased through the rule I was about to break, "two vacations a year. You, me, and Alvin. We'll go somewhere. We'll...go to a secluded beach, or...swim with dolphins, or whatever it is people do these days to have fun. I haven't thought it out," I rushed, "but I'm willing to compromise. *Come home.*"

Everleigh's eyes barely reopened, but there was a soft grin on her face. "You and dolphins. I hope I remember that when I wake up. Bram Whitlock swimming with dolphins. That's..." a yawn, "the funniest thing I think I've ever heard."

"Well, laugh about it over here. I can take care of you. I'll have the best doctors brought in to make sure you're okay."

"I'm not," she mumbled. "I'm not...okay."

"What do you mean? *Everleigh.*"

Her lids lowered, only to remain closed. The bed creaked, and I was suddenly being turned around to face the one man I'd threatened to destroy. I hated him for hurting my slave. I hated him with every ounce of evil inside me.

"Be blunt. How bad did you fuck her up?"

Hazel eyes flickered to the side and his voice was low as it came through. "Pretty bad."

"How bad? Has she been seen by a doctor? A surgeon? She could get an infection. *She could die.*"

"Mistress Harper has excellent care. A team has been flown in. What you saw was her medication kicking in. They're sterilizing a room now. I have it under control."

"Surgery then?"

"Maybe. They won't leave her side until she's well."

My head shook, and I couldn't stop from fisting my hair.

"You'll call the moment they're finished. I want to know how it goes. I want to know she's okay."

"I don't work for you, Mr. Whitlock. If my Mistress wants you to know how she is, she can tell you herself."

The phone went dead, and it took everything I had not to throw it against the wall. Instinct couldn't shake the feeling that there was something else—something neither of them were telling me.

AAMIR

*"**P**lease. I want to go home! Aamir!"*
 When I hadn't thought my life could get any worse, it had. *Whitlock.* There were no words or clear thoughts I could grasp to explain the torment my life had become. Before Jessa and I arrived, we were hooded and blinded. The ride was quiet, minus Jessa's sobs and pleas. When we finally stopped, we were pulled roughly and led in darkness down a maze that seemed to last forever. When our hoods were finally taken off, we stood among four guards in what looked like a hospital.

Just like the sea slaves on our passage to Red Island, the guards acted as if we were mute. As if they couldn't hear Jessa screaming out to me with everything she had. While she was taken in one direction in the medical department, I was practically dragged to the opposite side. Poked, prodded, tattooed...a vasectomy—that was what filled my first hours within the white walls of hell. I fought against the restraints. I yelled. Nothing mattered. By the time I was let go, I was so drugged up, I could barely wrestle the arms that dragged me to my new cell. *My new cage.* But this one was a room, with a door. A door with a window so small, all I could see were eyes peeking in on me every so often.

More time passed. A day. Two? I didn't know. If I were to go off the food they provided, it would only be two meals' worth. A stretch of hours. Dinner, and then breakfast? Was it close to lunch? My stomach growled, but I refused to think about how I'd been too out of it to eat. Dreams of escape consumed me. Even subconsciously, I knew I had to get out of here. But how?

*I could jump the guard. I could...*Mistress Harper's words came flooding back, overpowering my thoughts. *If you attempt to escape, they will kill you on the spot. Trust me when I say it is impossible, and not to even try. You will die.*

As much as I hated it, I knew she was right. I had seen the guards at almost every turn when they led me to my cell. This place was a massive maze. How would I get by them? I could kill them too, but then what? I didn't know my way out. The chances of me finding it before they found me were just as Mistress Harper had said: impossible.

"Jessa!"

Groaning, I eased from the creaky bed. I didn't make it a step before I stiffened through the massive ache in my balls. Sweat collected on my brow, and the pain had me trembling through the adrenaline brought on by the truth. *I'd never have kids.* I'd never see my child born, or hear them laugh, or get to experience the love knowing someone was completely mine—made from me. Even if I did escape, what if this was irreversible?

For minutes, I couldn't move as it all filtered through—our abduction, the ship, Red Island, being separated from my twin, arriving at Whitlock...the procedures, shots, tattoo. This wasn't a bad dream I'd wake up from. I was a sex slave. A male *sex slave*.

My brain couldn't fathom it. Sure, I had heard of human trafficking, but I had always assumed it was women and children. I was neither. I wasn't even a virgin. How big of a fool had I been? Had I been living under a rock my entire life? Sea slaves, sex slaves, an island housing imprisoned human beings, fortresses, twisted men who paid to end us all…why was there not more news or information about this in the real world? Why was this not projecting through every television in every single home? This wasn't a one-country problem. This was a world epidemic. A tragedy. People's children were being taken and used for the sick needs of evil men. And then they were being killed. I didn't understand how any of it was possible. Didn't our government know how bad this had truly become? Didn't other countries' governments know? *They had to.* The men who ran these places, they weren't slippery, disgusting creatures. Not on the outside. From what I could tell, they were rich and sophisticated —*educated* with their proper grammar and multiple languages. They had planes, guards, and servants. They had taxes for fuck's sakes. They had to have been monitored. Weren't they? Or was I wrong? Were they above the system? Were *they* the system?

My mind raced through every torturous step I took. This wasn't over. This wasn't the end of me. I was a fighter. I had always been a fighter. I had to do something. Somehow, some-way, I'd get out of here and find Layla, and then I'd bring this place and Red Island down. It was the only way I could prevent this from happening to others.

A loud pop sounded, and I jolted to a stop next to an empty bed as the bolt slid back and my door opened. Pounding erupted in my chest and I tensed, preparing myself as a guard took a step inside.

"Got your dinner." He paused, easing the tray a few inches toward me. "You want to come get it, or do you want me to put it down?"

"Is it poisoned?"

Thick brown eyebrows drew in to highlight darker eyes. The man looked to be in his early forties. His hair was thin, but he didn't appear old by any means. He was built, and of average size.

"I think we both know it isn't poisoned. Why would you have gone through all of this only to be killed so soon? You haven't even made it to the auction. If anything, you're eating better than the guards. Organic, and all that shit. We have the same foods, but we tend to stick to pizza and burritos at the cafeteria." He paused. "Are you going to take this?"

Just breathing in the aroma of grilled meat, my hunger won. Loud growling sounded between us, and he looked toward the white gown covering my stomach. Heat burned my cheeks, and he edged the tray closer.

"Go ahead. Take it."

I was starving. *Bread.* It was all I had eaten for weeks. This was meat, I could smell it, and my body new what it needed.

I took a step, wincing as I uneasily looked the man up and down. He wasn't being a dick, or silent, like the others had been. He was talking. Almost nice. If I could continue to get him to talk, or think of me as something more than a slave, maybe...

"Thank you." I took the tray, hesitating in putting distance between us. "You mentioned the auction. Is that what's next? I mean, will I have to go back to the hospital for anything else? A foot removal or something?"

He laughed. "No. Just the tour and auction."

"Tour?"

"That's right. Our Main Master will lead you around the grounds. He'll show you where you can go, and where you can't."

Hope flourished. "How soon is that?"

"The tour? A day before the auction. You still have a few weeks."

"Weeks?" My voice cracked as I glanced around the small white room.

"This isn't so bad. Soak in the time, slave. Being bought might not work out so well for you. It usually doesn't for most men."

My mouth opened, only to shut. I didn't want to know what he meant. I couldn't if I was going to focus on getting out of here. And I needed to focus.

"Just knock on the door when you're finished. I'll pick up your tray."

"Will you be outside for a while?"

The guard's lips tightened. "Until the end of my shift. Got about five hours left, give or take."

"Will you be back tomorrow? Or the next day?"

There was hesitancy as he gave a swift nod and pulled the door shut behind him. Silence once again closed in around me and I groaned as I headed to sit on the bed. My hands were shaking as I hovered above the thick lid covering the plate. A package of plastic utensils rested next to a small cup. I couldn't get over how it looked like a hospital tray. He'd mentioned cafeteria. This place was too well equipped. It added to the unease of how smoothly this operation ran, not to mention just how big this place really was.

Two small chicken breasts sat on one edge of the plate, along with rice and a mix of broccoli and cauliflower. It didn't matter that I rarely ate vegetables. My fingers were already tearing into the package and I began to pop them in my mouth as fast as I could. Flavors burst over my tongue anew, awakening my senses to a state I could barely believe. Weeks of flavorless food left me hyper-sensitive as I swallowed and tore into the chicken. I was ravenous, and suddenly…guilt-ridden. Was Layla eating this well? Was the Dragon feeding her more than bread? That's all we'd gotten while I was trapped in his dungeon with her.

My chewing slowed as I stared at the door. Swallowing was almost impossible, but I forced the rest of my meal down. Guilt wouldn't prevent me from being as strong as I needed to be. I had to escape. I had to rescue my twin.

SCOUT 19

J had gone through a lot in my years at Whitlock. I'd been an early recruit thanks to my grandfather. Our legacy was in the foundation of the fortress, going back many generations from when Whitlock first opened. But the money wasn't in our family anymore. If I wanted to be honest in terms of Whitlock status, my grandfather shouldn't have even been allowed access. He had one slave throughout his time here—one he beat and carved into like a Thanksgiving turkey. But he didn't kill her. He kept her alive to carry on our name, and to allow me a place in a world I would never truly belong. Ol' man Whitlock knew it too, and still granted me access regardless that the slave had died from sepsis only weeks before my admittance. It didn't matter to him. I was offered an ultimatum. The cost to be here was simple compared to what I faced in the real world with my pill-popping, abusive mother and dead father—my life.

Whitlock was mine on one condition: I gave myself over to it. I could live here. I could work here. I could even buy a slave if I ever acquired the money. It was an offer too good to pass up. So, I left everything behind and trained, where I eventually became a guard amongst the white. White walls. White floors. The wrong color for the evil deeds I had been introduced to. Fighting came naturally, and my upbringing made the violence feel like home.

Two years as a guard, and I put in my request for scout. I didn't expect it to be accepted the first time. It was rare one so young was thrown on the streets for such a risky operation, but I didn't give up. Six months later, when the solicitation came out again, I reapplied, and amazingly, I'd made it. At twenty, on the streets, I caught onto the game quickly. My age, coupled with my decent looks, helped me traffic just the right number of girls to keep me in good standing. At twenty-three, I was getting damn good. I was also in the one place I didn't think I'd return to until after my new mission: the scout safehouse, half an hour outside Chicago.

The gate squeaked, and I rolled the window down, nodding to the guard who controlled the underground entrance. For such a dirty operation, the house was impeccable. Sitting at the end of a secluded street, the two-story white colonial appeared picturesque with its grand columns and finely trimmed hedges. To anyone who watched, upper-class normalcy thrived. Little did they know, the retired Marine First Sergeant who occupied the place was anything but.

Three, as we referred to him, was as perverse as they came. White-gloved, clean interior marked every inch of the mansion, but our leader was messy in his actual work downstairs. There were many times we had to double up on girls because the first wouldn't make it to Whitlock. It was also why we didn't report our chosen until we were sure she'd arrive at her intended destination. Three could be a loose cannon. There were times he went weeks without obliterating our list. Then, times like this…no slave was safe.

I put the car in park, taking in two scouts smoking by the

large metal door. Given their scowls and posture, I knew what was going on inside. It left me throwing the door open as I climbed out.

"Where the fuck have you been? I've been calling for hours." Pulling my phone free from the pocket of my leather jacket, I flashed it toward Six. "Business. I've only come to get my stuff."

"You're leaving?"

Both scouts looked at each other before Eight dropped the butt of his cigarette and ground it under the heel of his steel toe.

"That's right. I'm on the elaborate hunt. I fly out in a few hours."

"You're kidding me."

"I don't kid. You know that."

Six and Eight moved out of my way as I continued toward the door, their feet heavy as they followed. The moment I opened the barrier, the echoing screams were automatic. My lips tightened, and I went down a few cells before I slowed. They quickly moved in close.

"How the fuck did you get in? I didn't think the Main Master was accepting anymore scouts?"

"He's not."

"Then why you? You're the youngest here. No offense, but—"

"How many?"

I stepped to the door, glancing through the small window toward the top. A slave stood in the center of the room, restrained by hanging cuffs. Crimson covered the lower half of her face, and her nose looked to be crushed. A wild excitement lit Three's eyes as he circled around the young girl. Ringlets were wild around her, down past her nude, olive shoulders, and the closest strands were matted with blood.

"How many?" I repeated, glancing back to Six and Eight.

Six shook his head, his dark hair swaying around his shoulders. When he pursed his thin lips, I knew it wasn't good.

"He's on his fourth since you left. We'll be lucky to salvage the other two. My guess is they'll be dead before dawn."

"Son of a bitch. I don't have time for this shit." My curse was drowned out by a shriek. It ended with a solid pop. But it wasn't from a hit. I knew all too well where Three was in his torturing process.

Elbow?"

Nodding at Eight, I glanced through the glass. Screams were deafening as our leader reached up and snapped her pinky finger. It stuck out to the side in an odd angle. The horrified, pain-filled expression as she sucked in a breath had his free hand diving to the dark curls between her legs. His shoulder surged forward, and her legs thrashed to find footing. She was short, making the effort useless. With his other hand, he reached for her ring finger. *Snap.*

I didn't wait. My fist banged against the door angrily. Stepping back, Six threw me a glare. I knew I was going to piss Three off by cutting his playdate short, but I didn't give a shit. The rest of the scouts were going to have to deal with it. The Main Master might need me before my allotted time, and I was going to be there if that were the case.

Metal banged and bounced from the wall as our leader surged through the threshold.

"What the fuck do you want? You better have a damn good fucking excuse for interrupting me, boy."

"I do. I'm leaving."

"Leaving where?"

Standing tall, I didn't back down as he got inches from my face.

"I've been issued orders. I need you to sign me out and send the release to Mateo so he knows I've gone through the required steps."

"Document? *Right now?*"

"I'm afraid so. The Main Master is in a bit of a hurry. I don't think you'd want to upset him."

Three's glare went to the cell, and then back to me. "Why are you telling me this? Mateo would have called me if you were chosen. You were not. The selection was made weeks ago."

"It was, but that's irrelevant. I'm chosen now. You can call Mateo if you don't believe me."

Suspicion crept onto his face as he grabbed his phone from his pocket. The moment he clicked the button, his expression transitioned to worry. Again, he looked toward the door as he brought the phone to his ear.

"You called, sir?"

"*Hours ago.*" The scout leader's loud voice boomed through. It was early. The flight from Cheyenne to Chicago had been a few hours, then the drive, not to mention I had to tidy stuff up at Whitlock before I managed to leave. I hadn't taken that into account, but I didn't care. Mateo knew his job, and we were both on the Main Master's clock.

"Sorry, I didn't hear my phone. Were you calling about Scout Nineteen? I have him here. He mentioned something about a release paper."

"Maria Warner! Maria Warner! Help! Help me, please!"

Pleas broke out from the room, and Three reached over, slamming the barrier shut before stomping down the hall. Following, I gave a nod to the guys as they whispered to each other. The girl was as good as gone. She'd never make it to Whitlock. She wouldn't make it out of that room alive given Three's angry stride to the stairs.

"Yeah, I know it. Been awhile since I had to get into that folder. I'll email it right over."

A curse followed as he hung up. The door was thrown open to the main level and he waved me away without so much as looking back. Shaking my head, I headed toward my room. The wooden stairs creaked under my feet and the fake pictures on the wall drew my attention as I headed up. The family that smiled back was nothing more than for show. Yet, here, in this moment, I questioned who they were. It was stupid, but something I couldn't push away. My mother had never looked that happy. Not once that I could remember. And the two children sitting by the woman...they were equally as enthusiastic. It was foreign to understand that sort of emotion. Why I had never contemplated it before was beyond me. Why I was even letting it in now was more bizarre. I was so close to making something of myself. Maybe that was the conundrum. I never thought I'd actually stand a chance at being someone within Whitlock. Now, I could.

Footsteps sounded only a moment before Twenty-four broke around the hall. He jerked to a stop, smiling.

"Where the fuck have you been? We had plans to go to Borders last night."

I rounded the turn as he followed me down the hall. When I opened my door, the desolate space had me coming to a stand-still. My room didn't look like the other scouts. They had tables with weapons strewn out. Some even had posters on their walls. The space I claimed as my own was just as empty as it had been when I moved in years ago.

"Whitlock called. I've been assigned to the search. I leave immediately."

"What? You're fucking kidding me."

Glancing at Twenty-four, I shook my head as I opened my closet and began gathering my clothes.

"Do you know where you're going?"

"No." Intentionally, I paused before grabbing my suitcase from the corner of the walk-in space. "I did overhear something about Ecuador in the lounge. Maybe they'll send me there."

"Fuck." The word dragged out as he lowered to the edge of the bed. "You know if she's there..." Silence had me looking over.

"I know. You don't have to worry."

"Let's not play the tough-guys. I'm serious. Everleigh Harper is dangerous. Her men are dangerous. You can't drop your guard for a second. Not one."

I threw him a smile as I tossed the suitcase on the foot of the bed.

"I'll be fine."

"Don't be so sure of that. I've seen her. *I know her.* If she's there and knows you're after her, you will not be fine. She will kill you, Nineteen." Twenty-four paused, lacing his fingers as he stared at the floor. "I was a guard for a while. You know that. Well, I was pulling duty when she was accused of killing her first Master. I stood next to the old high leader as Bram Whitlock had him chop off another guard's hand for hitting her." He glanced up. "Hitting her...*a slave.* I knew it then. I knew the Main Master loved her. We were never reprimanded for beating slaves back then. As long as it wasn't right before auction day, we could pretty much rough them up as much as we wanted. That day...everything changed. Maybe she would have been fine if it weren't for West Harper. Maybe the Main Master would have kept her in line as his slave. That didn't happen. West Harper fucked her up beyond repair. He created a monster bigger than the one living inside him. And now, Bram Whitlock wants her back. Fucking horrible mistake."

"You really think so? Some of the guards seem to like her."

As I put my clothes in my suitcase, my only real friend began a warning I knew I needed to heed.

"To confine that woman in a place where she can manipulate herself to full power—power over Whitlock and what it stands for...she'll change everything. Whitlock will be ash, and so will everyone inside it. Our Main Master is playing with fire. He thinks what he feels is love, and maybe it is, but let me ask you this. Can you love a void and expect it to love you back? Everleigh Harper is a shell. Action is all she knows. Emotion doesn't reside within that pretty package anymore. She's dead, Nineteen. She died long ago, and if the Main Master thinks he can revive what once was, he's mistaken. You can't keep a corpse and not expect it to rot. She will fester trapped within those walls. At least in the outside world, *she's free*. That's all she ever wanted."

BRAM

our days. Four days and not a word on my slave. I was sick with worry. Sick something bad happened and she was hurt even worse. Or dead. And who would tell me if something happened? Luke wouldn't. He didn't give a shit whether I knew. He only cared for her, and that filled me with even more fury.

I stared down the length of the large table at my members: Masters Hunt, King, Elliot, Barclane, and Torres—the men who were Whitlock's new foundation. I'd brought them in because of their amazing technological connections and pull in the outside world. They promised me Everleigh would be found within days. They were so confident. Weeks upon weeks later, they still couldn't deliver on their promise.

"So, you're telling me we had her exact fucking location on Red Island and none of you could track her whereabouts after she took off? Am I getting this right? Her jet didn't have secret powers or cloaking devices to make it invisible. It can't time travel. Yet...*nothing?*"

Hard faces stared at me silently. Master Hunt, my second, opened a file, refusing to look at me. "We have all the satellite

40

shots surrounding the time of her departure. None of the actual island. There's a block around it, just as there is here. But what we do have—"

"You are the director of the CIA, Master Hunt. You mean to tell me you couldn't turn off the device blocking the satellite's signal for…five minutes?"

Light gray eyes shot up to me. "No. We're all equally protected, Main Master. You know that. I could never, under any circumstance, turn it off. Even if I wanted to, I don't have that authority or any idea who does. No one was meant to know. It's a safeguard for all of us."

"What else do we have?" I snapped.

Barclane took the folder from Hunt, and walked over, handing me the file. There was a small stack of aerial shots: some boats, open ocean, nothing that stood out as a plane.

"What we do know is the plane arrived in Athens hours later. It hasn't left since. We're keeping a very close eye on it, but no one other than the pilots got off."

"So, she stopped somewhere else before they arrived. Have you backtracked their flight so you know where they flew in from?"

Master King nodded, opened his own file, and passed a paper to Barclane, who brought it to me.

"Three stops within Greece and the surrounding islands, Main Master. All three were…strategically placed. The airports were nothing more than a landing strip. Other than locations, we have no video or images of who got off."

"Of course you don't." I glared as I glanced at the different marked dots on the map. Back and forth, I went between the men and the paper. "Everleigh wouldn't know this on her own. When I find her, I'm recruiting her men. By God, if I ever want to disappear, you all don't stand a fucking chance at finding me! This is pathetic. I expected so much more out of all of you. Tomorrow, I better have some sort of news."

Standing, I spun and threw the door open as I headed back to my wing. For all the intel and money I was wasting, I was getting nowhere. My best hope rested on a slave—on the hope that Everleigh took my bait.

The two guards at my door stiffened as I rounded the corner, and I gave a nod as I swept through, heading inside. The quiet interior had me looking at my watch. It was noon—Alvin's nap time. Ms. Pat would be sitting with him. And me...I came to a stop, closing my eyes. I was exhausted. Sleep didn't come. It never really did to begin with, but especially not now that my obsession with my slave was out of control. I ached for her. My heart knew nothing but the need to have her back.

Walking into my bedroom, I slowed as I quietly shut the door and made my way to the bedside table. When I opened it, a smile tugged at my lips. Nothing was there, and that's what left me happy. The lotion and perfume I had made for Everleigh was gone. Once, I told her to wear it and know I was with her. And she'd taken it upon her return. *She'd taken me with her.* That meant something. It said everything she wouldn't.

I pushed the drawer closed and stripped off my suit jacket and tie. I barely had three buttons to my shirt undone before I couldn't resist the urge to pull my phone out and stare at the screen. Collapsing to the mattress, I compulsively hit her number. *Voicemail.* I didn't think as I hit the video calling. My entire body froze as it was accepted and Everleigh came in clear. She was sitting with the pillows all around her, and although her hair appeared brushed, she had dark circles under her eyes.

"Slave. I was worried. You never called. How did the surgery go? How do you feel? Are they taking good care of you?"

"I'm so mad at you, Bram Whitlock. If I were in my right mind, I wouldn't have answered the phone at all. *I can't believe you.*"

I pushed to sit against my own pillows as I soaked in her livid expression. She was so angry; she was on the verge of tears.

"I only wanted you to come back. I thought if you were drugged, I could explain things better. You'd listen, because you wouldn't have the choice to argue. I thought I could win you over before we arrived at Whitlock. I never imagined Luke hurting you."

"I'm pissed at the drugging, but that's not what I'm talking about. You separated my slaves. You gave the girl to the Dragon. Now, I hear you mean to sell the boy. Do you care *nothing* for what I want? For human life? Do you know what you've done to them?"

"I did what I had to do. Gavin Draper wanted her as the reward. Was I supposed to deny him—a Main Master who turned you in to me?"

"Yes! *They were mine.*"

"No, they were not. I didn't have a choice. If you would have just come home instead of going to Master Draper, he wouldn't have needed a reward. You could have bought them legally through the auction, and I would have supported you buying them. This isn't my doing, it's yours, Everleigh. You can't go behind my back and expect me to give you your way because I love you. You know better than that. You, more than anyone, know how Whitlock works."

"You've condemned those poor kids. You know that, and you don't care. You've never cared about anyone but yourself."

"That's also not true."

"*Yes, it is.* You say you love me, but you've never given me anything I've asked for, or wanted."

"Another lie. I let you leave. And *you once wanted me.* Do you remember that? You begged me to take you as my slave. Against my better judgement, I gave in. West ruined that, but we can have it again. We can make this work. And if you want slaves, I'll buy you however many you want. All you have to do is return. Our life doesn't have to be bad here. We'll have each other. *We'll have Alvin.*"

Blue eyes disappeared behind closed lids and dark hair

swayed over her shoulders as her head slightly lowered. The camera was trembling in her hold.

"A part of me wishes that could be true. That I could turn back time and..." A sniffle broke through. "Do you not see me? Do you not see what I've become?"

"Oh, I see. I told you I knew who you really were before you ever got on that plane. I don't care. You know me too. The entire reason I wouldn't take you as my slave is because I was afraid I would kill you. I'm still fearful of what I'm capable of, but I have to believe there's some reason things happened as they did. We're stronger than our demons. We can make this work."

"How?" Blue eyes blazed as they shot open. "We become a couple, raise a boy who is not ours, and pretend we're not surrounded by the same walls harboring the most malicious men on this planet? What if one of them hurts Alvin? What if they try to kill you again? Explain to me how that is a happily-ever-after?"

I pushed higher on the bed and licked my lips as my brain screamed to spout out an answer I knew was fabricated—to say anything to bring her home. I couldn't.

"Neither of us will ever have a fairytale. We're tragedy laced with love. Our best hope of happiness is with each other. I don't expect you to want this life. I know you don't but let me ask you this. Do you love me?"

The anger melted into pain as her features drew in. "I'll always love you."

"And do you think you'll be happier out there with who you are now? If I were to stop looking for you, and you had no scouts to sate your need, would the world be safe against the Everleigh who can't stop the urges to kill?" When she didn't reply, I continued. "We both know the answer to that. You belong here with me. You hate it, but it's the truth. The place you despise is the only home where you'll ever be safe. Where you'll ever experience the love you want. I can give you that. I can love you. I *do* love you."

"*I don't want to kill slaves.* If you think I'll ever give in and become one of those monsters of Whitlock, you don't know me at all."

A smile tugged at my mouth. "I never said anything about slaves. What I offer is much more your taste."

Her head rose, and her eyes flickered with interest. "What are you offering, Bram?"

"Your wildest dreams. I think it's high time we be honest and lay everything on the table. What do you say?"

"I say you're trying to convince me to come back at any cost. How do I know you'll be true to your word and not throw me in the White Room the moment I return?"

"You don't. This is where I ask you to trust me. And I'll trust you. Can you do that? Can you trust me, slave?"

Everleigh glanced above the phone, only to come back to me. I could tell someone had come into the room by the way her face became devoid of emotion. When the camera moved to rest angled against her propped-up legs, I caught a full glimpse of her silk pajama top and bandaged shoulder. She reached up, taking something from someone's hand. I knew it was pills when she brought her palm to her mouth and chased them down with water.

"Is there anything else I can get you, Ms. Harper?" *A woman's voice.*

"No, thank you. Please tell Luke I'll be fine and I wish not to be disturbed. I'll call him if I need anything."

"Yes, ma'am."

A slight sound of pain came as she shifted and brought the phone back up. From the glimpses I'd been given, I couldn't see anything that would trigger a possible location. There had been a small section of what looked like a wooden wall, but it could have been the headboard.

"I really hate that fucking name. *Harper*. I'd almost prefer you to go by Vicolette or Davenport, consequences be damned."

"Harper is who I am. I earned this name. It makes me happy knowing I killed the man who thought forcing it on me was the answer to all his problems."

"You were easy on him. He deserved to suffer for what he did to us. Now the woman I love carries a last name that makes my blood boil." I met her stare, frowning through the raw emotions. "I still can't believe he married you. I hate that he took something I never even thought conceivable. I was such a fool."

"You still can be at times. Take right now for instance."

"…What do you mean?"

Eveleigh's eyes rolled, and she looked away for a moment before coming back to me. At the slight blush on her cheeks, heat poured from my skin. I wanted her. I wanted her so much, my heart slammed into my chest. I could see the slave in her. See the Everleigh I fell in love with.

"We were talking about being honest. You want to lay out possible terms, fine. I'll take the bait and see what you have to say. I assume you mean to keep Alvin. To raise him as your heir so he can run Whitlock someday. Am I correct?"

"Yes."

"And you want us to be together. To be a family. Yes?"

I nodded, unable to stop the excitement at her even having this conversation with me. It seemed too much like my dreams instead of the game we had been playing.

"I can't be Everleigh Harper if we're a family, Bram. I refuse."

All I could hear was my pulse as it pounded in my ears. Swallowing was almost impossible. Surely, she couldn't mean what I thought she did. But if she was…

"Yes. Okay."

"I'm sorry?"

"You want me to marry you? I will. Right now."

Her mouth parted as she searched for what to say.

"You're having trouble believing me. Don't. If that's one of your terms for coming home, consider it done. I would have asked anyway. I think jumping right into it is the best thing we could do."

"I…I." She shifted. "You're not a marrying man."

"I wasn't, no, but I'm not the same person you left at Whitlock. I've had a lot of time to think. There's only one thing I know for sure and that's that we belong together. What better way to make you mine than marriage? It's simple really. I do want you as my wife, slave."

"No…you're lying. I don't believe you. You—"

"*Believe it.* You have always belonged to me. What's happened…it's my fault. Maybe if I would have given in all those years ago things would have been different. I can't change the past. All we can do is change the future. Marry me. Come home."

"It's not that easy."

"Sure it is. What else do you want? I'll give it to you. Just tell me."

The strong woman was melting away as she continued to search the room as if in a daze. She barely looked at me. Heavy breaths left her, and the phone went back to lean against her legs as she rubbed her eyes.

"I should go."

"Don't fight this. Be open with me. Tell me what it is you want."

"I shouldn't be talking while I'm on medication. I need to have a clear head. I can't think."

"There's nothing to think about. Nothing to be cautious of. We're just talking. You're telling me what you want so you can come home. Marriage. We both want it, but you have other things you need. I want to know what they are."

The rise and fall of her chest had my cock so hard, I could

barely break my gaze away from the way her nipples pushed through the thin material. *Wife. Wife.* Yes, I wanted her as mine. Everleigh Whitlock, my slave, my other half...for better or worst. The worst had already been here. She deserved better now, and I wanted to give it to her.

"You can't afford what I want."

"Afford? You want money?"

Blue eyes lowered back to me, and again, the phone rose. "No. My price is blood. Revenge."

"And you don't think I can afford to give you that? I'll paint these walls red with whoever it is you want to kill. Say the name. I'll deliver them to you wrapped in the same red ribbon you placed around the boxes you sent me."

Again, she grew quiet.

"It's that easy, slave. Give me the name. I'll have them brought in here right now so you can see I speak the truth. All you have to do is tell me you're on your way and we'll get this going. I'll even have a minister waiting."

"*It isn't that simple, Bram.* You make it sound like it is, but it's not. Yes, I have *names.* More than one. Lots. But I'm not finished with what needs to be done. I can't just grab my bags and fly to Whitlock."

"Okay," I said, calmly. "You're getting too upset. Just let me help."

"I can't trust you."

"You can. Listen to your heart, Everleigh. I'm in yours, just as you're in mine. *Trust. Me.* Tell me what you want me to do."

AAMIR

*T*he days were long, and the nights were even longer. I couldn't see the sun or moon, but I didn't need to in order to determine a schedule. Meals came on queue: breakfast, lunch, and dinner. Aside from that, nothing. Nothing but the confines of this cell. The walls were closing around me, and the routine did nothing to curb the psychotic thoughts causing me to constantly pace.

The guard who had talked to me before had been gone for days. The new ones wouldn't talk. They held their batons out, making me stay on the bed as they placed my tray just inside the door. Nothing. Nothing. Nothing…but my thoughts. My worry over Layla was killing me. What was my sister doing on Red Island? Where had the Dragon taken her when we were separated? The thought made me sick. If what the Main Master said was true, he would have taken her through his room to get to hers. Was he hurting her? Raping her?

Bile burned my throat, and I forced it down. A yell wanted to come at the flashes of her lying there unconscious and hurt. And me…over her. Fucking her—my own sister. I hadn't wanted to, and I almost became just as sick as I felt now while I was being

forced to do it. That hour, or hours—however many there were—
ate at me. They melted through every sense of self I had left. I
wasn't good. Somehow, through the crazed thoughts of blood
and violence that looped in my mind, I knew that.

*Deeper, slave. Fuck her! Fuck her pussy hard, just like you
know you've always wanted to.*

The giant's taunts overwhelmed me, forcing a yell to explode
from my mouth. I spun, heading to the opposite side of the room
faster. Heavier.

*Oh, yeah. Just like that. You got it. Now, if you could only
stop crying. Cry baby. I bet you're still on your momma's tit too.
Mommy. I'd fuck your mother. Right in front of you. I bet you'd
want to fuck her too!*

Laughter from all the sea slaves echoed around me. Heat
blistered my skin and a gag mingled with my yell as it turned
into a roar. Faster, I walked, eating up the floor with every swift
step. My fists opened and jerked back in, squeezing tight.

My heavy breaths became his as he came up from behind,
wrapping his large hands around my hips and pushing them
forward to make me go faster. *You feel her gripping around your
cock? Faster. Faster. Come in her. Fill her up good.*

Foreign chants. More laughter. I could barely stay hard, let
alone reach an orgasm. Time dragged on. Repeatedly, I tried to
fight him off so I could stop. It only had the giant pushing the
blade of a knife against Layla's throat. An eternity stretched out
and my eyes tried to close. Anything to make reality disappear.
He didn't let me block it out. He made me finish. And finish, I
had. Though, not inside her like he'd wanted. I couldn't bear
that. I couldn't risk it. Layla may have been on birth control, but
I wasn't sure, and just the thought of an accident sickened me
even more.

"On the bed."

Memories vanished, and I blinked hard, turning to view the
guard. Slowly, he placed the tray down.

"I need to shower. I need to get out of here."

"Showers are on Tuesdays and Fridays."

"How far away is that?"

Eyebrows drew in as the dark-skinned man stared at me.

"Tomorrow."

"Is that Tuesday or Friday?"

"It's shower day. That's all you need to know."

The door slammed shut, and my eyes closed. Screaming out in anger was almost impossible. Ignoring the food, I continued, back and forth. I couldn't eat. Not with the images that wouldn't stop.

"Look at her arch. Can you feel how wet she is at you being inside her? I think even unconscious, she knows you're fucking her. You like that, don't you, slave? You like fucking your sister. I like it."

I was going to be sick. I was...

My steps faltered, and I didn't have to stick my finger down my throat to become ill. The disgusting pleasure rolled over me like a breaking dam and I heaved, once, twice. I let the vomit cover my chest as I cemented myself to the cold floor and collapsed to my knees. They hit with crushing impact, but I felt no pain. I felt nothing but the disgust over what I had done.

"Ahhh! No! No!" Again, hot vile poured over me between my spouts of uncontrollable denial. To lean forward came naturally, but what I had done was anything but. I forced my head back, letting the liquid cover my skin. I was past the point of caring about keeping myself clean. I didn't deserve to spare myself from my sins. I was filthy and sick in more ways than physical. To even associate pleasure was wrong...yet my mind, my body, made me remember. It made me experience it when the twisted sensations shouldn't have been there.

"Ahhhhh! Ah!"

Layla's full lips opened in a ragged breath, and I was fucking her again while staring down in what I knew was horror. But something else was there. Love? She *was* my twin. How could I not love her? But that shouldn't have been there. There were so many emotions, and they were all morphing together and driving me crazy. They were burning and eating at every part of me.

"You like it. You like it. You like it."

"No! Stop. *Stop it!"*

Knuckles crunched as my fist slammed into the cement. Once I started, I couldn't stop. That deep cackling laughter vibrated in my ears, moving through my body like a tuning fork. The hum hit just as hard as I began to hit the Giant's face. Warmth grew at the continual impact. Warmer. Hotter.

"I'll kill you! I'll fucking...*kill you*. I'm going to. I will!"

"Hey!"

"I hate you! Hate! Kill! You!"

"Get down! Get the fuck down!"

Hands were suddenly pushing at my shoulders from behind to flatten me. My elbow locked, but blood and bile had me sliding forward. Before I could process what was going on, instinct kicked in. Digging my fingers into the bicep behind me, I rolled, taking the guard down beneath me. I knew it wasn't the Giant, but his face kept coming. *Her face...his face.*

I was hitting again. Punching the guard so fucking hard, his face was caving under the blows. Years of training fueled me until the meaning of life no longer existed. He was my enemy, just like everyone at this place. The guards, the Main Master, the Dragon, the Giant. They were all the same. Evil. Sick. Evil.

Gurgling sounded, muffling under the choking. Fingers loosened on my white robe, and I couldn't stop myself from knocking the weak grip free before I drove my fist even harder into the mush at the center of his face. His leg kept twitching while his body jerked and swayed.

"Beson, report."

I slowed, somehow stopping, mid-swing. Repeatedly, I blinked through all the blood covering my hands.

"Beson, stop fucking with the blues. Report."

Scrambling back, I couldn't stop my heavy breaths. Dark red pooled underneath his head and his legs spasmed. He didn't look like he was breathing, but I couldn't be certain.

"Beson."

Annoyance was turning into concern from the voice over the guard's radio. My eyes scanned the room, stopping on the door. It was closed, but if he was in here, it wasn't locked.

Clawing the cement, I raced for the door, jerking the heavy metal open. What faced me had my already racing heart exploding. Fear hadn't been there before, only anger. The devoid emotion was all I felt as I let go of the door and began walking back into the room. The barrel of the gun stayed level with my face, and three men in dark uniforms glared, glancing toward the guard on my floor as they entered my cell.

"Damn shame," one mumbled. "Damn, damn shame."

"I…" Swallowing hard, I circled around as the men came even closer.

"I say we put a bullet between his eyes and be done with it."

"And let him off so easily?" The one with the gun shook his head. "No fucking way."

"He'll pay. Injuring or killing a guard is a White Room offense."

"White Room, yes." The gun was thrust at the smallest guard. "But not before this motherfucker pays for what he did to Beson. Mike, go check on him. I'll take care of this slave."

"*H*e's where?"

I grunted the question, my teeth clenching through the painful buzz of the tattoo gun vibrating my sternum. Each number was swift—a false identification for the slave I represented. A necessity for my mission.

"He killed a guard. The slave is pretty beat up because of it, but alive. He's in the White Room. That's where you're going."

"*Great*. How'd he manage that? The guard should have known better than to get too close without backup."

"There was vomit on the floor. I assume he went to check on Eleven, then the slave attacked."

"Is the slave sick?"

Mateo's head shook, even though he shrugged. "Hasn't been since he was put in a few hours ago. A ploy, nerves, we'll never know. The guards will be gunning for him though, you can bet your ass on that. Your job is to keep him alive without revealing who you are. Why the Main Master wants him spared is beyond me, but he does."

I winced through the nine as the needles rounded along the

upper curve. "I'll do my best. What if I'm recognized? I know a decent amount of guards."

"Use your imagination. This isn't my mission, it's yours." Mateo checked his watch before stepping toward the door. "You'll be in the room next to his. If I get any news, I'll let you know. Don't die during one of those red lights." He grasped the door knob, then paused. "Which reminds me. *A tip.* Try to bunker the two of you down in a room when the blood-spill begins. There's a slave in one of those cells who's making quite a name for herself. She's got a taste for killing, and she's good at it."

"She? A woman?"

A smile appeared, lasting a few seconds before he shifted on his feet. "It's debatable, I guess. Woman…girl. She's on the younger side."

"Younger side? You want me to be cautious of a child? A girl child at that?"

"Are we not cautious of Everleigh Harper? You should know by now sex means nothing if it's paired with brains. You'd be smart not to underestimate this one. The guards don't. They've been betting on the body count. Just steer clear. I don't want to have to explain to the Main Master why you or the damned slave are dead because of a *'girl child'.*"

The door slammed behind Mateo, and I rested my head back as something was slid over my chest and bandaged.

"He's right, you know. Forty-two may be young, but she's not someone I'd want to cross."

I glanced up at the bald tattoo artist, my lips pursed. He was on the smaller side and maybe a hundred and forty pounds soaking wet, but he was a man. To hear him say that about a child had my curiosity piqued.

"What do you know about this girl?"

Nervous eyes wouldn't look at me as he cleaned up. I put on the white hospital gown, standard for the White Room, as I waited for him to talk. He wanted to. It was in the way he kept looking over at me.

"I tattooed her long ago. I wouldn't normally remember a number or face, but I remember her. She was only eight months old. She was the first baby I ever tattooed."

"Eight months? She's an old slave then, back when Ol' Master Whitlock reigned?"

"That's right. She's probably around fourteen now. A child in most eyes—a veteran by Whitlock standards." A snort sounded as he turned toward me. "No clue what the hell she went through growing up here, but whatever it was, it was bad enough for her to kill her daddy."

"Daddy?"

"Well, stepdad, technically, but her father, nonetheless. He was nearing hysteria the night he came in with the little girl. Blood covered his clothes. It was smeared on the side of his face and drenched on one side of his head. I remember it was thick in his hair. Maybe he was injured. I don't know. He was crying while begging the old Main Master. Said he had nowhere to keep the girl. He wanted the world to think her dead like the mother. Something about his career. The man threw out numbers like he had all the money in the world. Suppose he did because Whitlock agreed. I never saw them after that. Didn't even really remember the girl until I heard the story of a powerful Master being killed by his slave. The number. I'll never forget it. Everything came back to me then, and it wasn't long before more murders circulated the cafeteria about her White Room massacres."

The door opened, and I glanced back at two guards. I didn't recognize them, but I could sense their anger as a pale, younger guy clamped onto my arm.

"That's what I fucking said. Bullshit if you ask me."

"Did they tell you why?"

"Of course not, but I'm not stupid. They need guards after that bitch's break-in. It's her fault they rejected my application."

"Who?"

An older guard in what looked to be his late thirties paused in almost disbelief at my question. Before I could internally smile, the back of his hand connected against my cheek with a force that snapped my head to the side. Red flashed in my vision while rage rolled inside. I kept it at bay, knowing I couldn't walk into the White Room without some form of abuse. Especially, if my story was going to be believable.

"Did I fucking hear you right? Did you just speak to us, *slave*? Keep your mouth shut and your ears closed, or I'll cut them off. You hear nothing. *You see or say nothing.*"

Grabbing my other arm, he jerked, dragging me to the door. The younger guard's grip tightened on my bicep as they pulled me out and down the hall at a fast pace. Blood trickled from my nose, over my lip, feeding the buried anger.

"That bitch isn't willingly coming back. She can't. Weren't you listening to the high leader at the meeting?"

"Sure, but what's he going to do? The Main Master will find her. She can't hide forever. One of these days someone is going to capture her, and when they do, she'll go right back to being a slave."

"Newbie," the older guard grumbled. "You don't know shit. You weren't even here when she was."

"That doesn't matter. It's obvious the Main Master is searching for her because he loves her. The high leader can say whatever he wants. When it comes down to it, the Main Master will get his girl and keep her under lock and key. Then, we can finally move on. I'm sick of all this. She's all anyone talks about. Everleigh this, twenty-four-six-ninety that. I hear that fucking number in my dreams. I can't stand it anymore."

"Well, you don't have a choice."

The hall turned, and I kept my head down as we passed a pair of guards. Minutes dragged on while we lifted in elevation through the Whitlock maze. The guards continued to bicker, but I stayed in my head. Despite the training I'd received over the years, the White Room was no joke. No one was going to have my back. If someone came after me, it was kill or be killed. I had never been in the red lights, but I had pulled enough guard there I hadn't missed the free-for-alls on the monitors.

"Got another one for you."

My eyes rose to connect with a pair of light green ones. Albert's head cocked, and he licked his lips, pausing before he brought his attention back to the men restraining me.

"Stick him in the holding room. I'll have the slave put in the system."

A side door opened, and I was shoved inside the ice-cold space. Only moments passed before my former friend barged in. We hadn't spoken since I became a scout, but we hadn't separated on bad terms either.

"Well?"

Rubbing my forearm under my nose, I could feel the blood smear across my face. "Well, what? I'm a slave."

"And I'm a Master. Is that how it is, or did you fuck up on the outside world?"

"No fuck-ups. I'm just a slave." I tugged down the hospital gown exposing the small tattoo at the center of my chest. "Slave Nineteen, actually."

Eyes widened as he let out a deep exhale. "That far, huh? Must be some serious shit going on." At my silence, he continued. "Okay, Slave Nineteen, let's get you to your room."

"You can't tell them," I said, lowly. "No one can know who I am."

"No one will."

"If they figure it out…"

"You're a slave," Albert said, sternly.

"Thanks."

"You won't be thanking me come tonight."

"Red light?"

Silence, this time from him.

"I see," I breathed out.

"Nah, I don't think you do. Stay out of the hall if you can help it."

"The girl? This, forty-two?"

Leaning forward, Albert kept his voice down. I knew there were cameras on us, but I was praying they were more focused on the hall full of cells than me.

"The girl is good, but she does not fight alone. She has followers. Men who not only protect her but supply her victims in this sick game she now plays. We used to go in. You know, stress relief, that sort of thing. Not anymore, man. When the hall goes red, we're content watching the action from the screens."

"Who puts the prisoners back in their cells when it's over?"

Albert's face hardened. "We go in then, but they know better. We've had to put our authority there. When the red light goes off, they return. If they remain in the halls by the time their doors lock shut, they die. Bullet, right to the head. We had to set the example early. They were smart to listen."

"You kill them? What if it's not their fault they get locked outside?"

"Hey, I don't make the rules. Whoever is not in their cell when those doors bolt, dies. Be smart. Keep your ass in your room."

"I'm not sure I can do that."

My words came out almost inaudible. Before Albert could reply, another guard entered.

"Everything good here?"

Pressure gripped around my arm as Albert led me to the door. "Yep. Just going over the rules with the new slave. We're done. You can take him to his room."

BRAM

"*J*ust leave it and shut the door behind you."

The anger in my tone couldn't be disguised. I sat at my desk seething, wishing there was a way to get Everleigh to open up to me. She wouldn't. Our conversation hadn't lasted but two minutes longer before she pulled the plug and hung up. I shouldn't have pushed her, but I couldn't help it. Couldn't she see? Yes, she saw. It was the entire reason she ended our conversation. She was close—so close, it was scaring the shit out of her.

"Main Master?"

My gaze lifted from the document I had been staring at for the last twenty minutes. What it held, I couldn't even remember. I didn't want to. All I wanted was her.

"Didn't I tell you to put it down and leave?"

Derek frowned, and I only realized he wasn't holding anything anymore. A deep exhale left me as I sat straighter. "I'm sorry, what is it?"

"You can't keep going on this way. I've been waiting for a reply on slave twenty-seven-eleven, and I have yet to get your orders."

"Eleven? What about Eleven?"

The high leader paused, his lips tightening in what I knew was disappointment and worry. "He requires a board, Sir."

"A board? For what?"

More hesitation—weariness? I studied my most trusted man, trying to get a read on the situation.

"He killed a guard. Currently, he's in the White Room, but he must face the board for his crime."

"He killed a guard? Shit." My eyes closed. Another dilemma to deal with concerning my future wife. In her eyes, Eleven was her slave, and I had hoped to keep it that way. The scout was meant to protect the boy—to room with him until the tour and keep him safe in case I got Everleigh back before the auction. But murder? I couldn't publicly excuse that. "The board has more important things to deal with right now. Give him ten lashes and put him back in his cell."

"But...*Main Master*, I can't do that."

"I beg your pardon?"

"Whitlock rules state if a slave commits murder he is either to live his days in the White or die. He can't be punished and returned to his cell. He may kill again. Next time, it could be a Master."

"If he murders again, he will face death. I need him at the auction." Each word came out through clenched teeth. "I have Mistresses now, remember? I need all the men I can get."

"I'm sorry, but I can't break the rules. You know I can't. The Whitlock Bible is law. What do we have if not that?"

Me. My rules. I wanted to say it but held my tongue as defiance and loyalty twisted my gut for all the wrong reasons. Derek was true to Whitlock, where secretly I had been hoping he'd place his alliance with me. Before my change in behavior, he had. Or maybe I was just a better outcome at the time than West and he'd always been devoted to Whitlock.

"You're right. His behavior does not excuse conveniences. I

have a lot on my mind with these new Mistresses. I wasn't thinking," I said, smiling and standing. "That's why I have you. Keep
him in the White while I meet with the board. We'll decide his
fate tonight. I'll let you know."

Derek bowed before turning and leaving my office. The
moment the door shut, I couldn't contain the growl or need to
slam my fist into the desk. Whitlock was a mess. *I* was a mess.
So much so, I grabbed my phone. The need to call Everleigh was
unbearable. Anger had me squeezing it until suddenly...it rang.
The action made me stiffen as my gaze lifted to the camera I kept
recording my office.

"*You're watching me.*"

"And you're looking in the wrong direction. You have to get
him out of there. *Now.*"

"How do you propose I do that? You were listening. Your
slave is gone, Everleigh. I can't get him back."

"Yes, you can. You're the Main Master."

"Everleigh..." Collapsing back in my chair, my head lowered
to rest against my free hand.

"Bram, if you don't remove him from the White Room, he
may die. You said this was my fault. You're right, it is. I should
have never gone to the Dragon, but I did. I can't change that.
What I can do is ask you to save him. Please. For me."

To speak was impossible while duty and love battled. The
answer was easy. The consequences were not.

"Are you coming home yet?"

"I already told you, I can't. I have things I need to do."

"Then let me see your face while you talk to me."

A pause, then ringing refilled the room. I hit the video button,
feeling myself relax as blue eyes stared at me pleadingly. The
rage subsided, transitioning into my obsessive longing.

"There's my slave. Tell me more of your plan. Let me help
you, and I'll see what we can do about Eleven. There might be

something...*if you can open up to me.* Just a little. That's all I ask."

"That's blackmail."

"A little blackmail never hurt anyone."

"It hurts me. I'm asking for your help to save a boy's life."

The sadness in her soft tone had my slight grin disappearing. "I said I'll see what I can do."

"You mentioned a meeting tonight. Will you meet with the board to discuss him?"

"I will."

"And what do you think they'll say?"

My smile returned. "They'll say whatever I want them to say."

"No. I don't believe they will this time." The black slip glided over Everleigh's chest as she moved along the bed and stood. When she began to walk, I soaked in everything around her. There was a table with two red velvet chairs. The walls were wooden...but not like a cabin. A window. *Water.*

"You're on a boat."

"What?" She jerked to a stop, twisting her mouth as her head turned to the side to gaze across the ocean. "I believe they're called yachts. And that's not your concern, Bram. We're talking about Eleven and the board."

"I told you I'll take care of it. I want to talk about us and your plans."

Suddenly, a screen from a laptop was in view and she was gone. The annoyance hit hard until I realized what she was showing me. Multiple different screens were up, some with Masters walking around their apartments, others were maps.

"How did you get all that?"

"We'll discuss that later. What I want you to see is your board members. One in particular. The top of the screen shows a map. There's a flashing dot. That would be Master Hunt, your second. As we speak, he is in D.C. Do you know what he is doing there?"

I opened my mouth, but nothing would come. I had no idea.

"Right now, he is leaving a meeting with top government officials. He's going to get in his car and drive to a late lunch at a restaurant called Dos Hombres. Nothing too fancy. He'll dine alone but run into an acquaintance while he's there. Afterward, he'll hop on a plane back to Whitlock and arrive a little after nine, your time. That's what anyone would see if they were tracking him. Do you want to know what he's really up to?"

Hard pounding thudded against my chest. Nothing short of amazement made it almost impossible to speak. "I do."

The camera turned back to Everleigh. She was walking again. When she stopped, she bit her lip and sat on the edge of the bed.

"When Master Hunt is halfway through his lunch, someone will wave at him from across the restaurant. It'll look as though they're old friends who just happen to run into each other. Master Hunt will ask him to sit, and they'll smile and move in to talk quietly, as if they're reminiscing of the old days. What they're really doing is confirming a shipment of slaves arriving in Japan a week from now."

"Japan?" I shook my head as my mind began putting together possible reasons. "He's the CIA director. He overlooks more than just Whitlock. I already knew that."

"You know more than you'll admit to yourself. Bram…"

"No." I forced a grin. "I'm not worried about it. Is this part of your plan? To monitor and foil Master Hunt's plans, whatever they may be?"

"I'm not a fool. I can't take on every Whitlock around the world. My concern is over the one I call home, and the man who runs it. You're smarter than this. Think. What all do you know about the men in your new circle? What do you *really* know? Aside from their connections and qualifications, I don't believe you looked too hard into their past or present. That scares me, and it should scare the hell out of you as well."

"You fear for no reason. Once you return, this will all be over."

"We both know that's a lie. My return will mark the beginning, not the end. You don't tease lions and pretend their appetite will wane. These Masters are in a feeding frenzy, high on the blood *you've* allowed them to shed. They must be reeled in. You can do that tonight. Call off my search and start monitoring the monsters you've created before it's too late."

"Too late for whom? You? They're so close, slave. We both know it."

"The only one who seems to know anything around here, *Master*, is me. Up your game. If you can't focus enough to run your fortress without me there, I can't trust you enough to keep me and Alvin safe when I return. Prove the Master I fell in love with is still alive in you somewhere. Take back control, find yourself, and see the truth happening all around you. Save my slave. Put those Masters in place by any means necessary. Do that, and I may be home sooner than you think."

At the video going dark, a roar tore from my throat. Was she still there? It didn't show the call as disconnected. "*Everleigh.* Slave!" Nothing. "Woman, so help me, you better show me your face."

Challenging eyes returned. The woman I loved was there, her stare cutting right into the core of who I was. It picked me apart in ways I couldn't begin to decipher.

"Where are you, Master? I need you. *We all need you.*"

"Don't play games with me. I'm right here where I've always been."

"No...the man I'm talking to is not Bram Whitlock. If he were, he'd already be pulling up his Masters on the computer and searching for the warnings he's been given." She paused as my eyes flickered to the black screen of my monitor. "That's right. Move the mouse."

My jaw tightened as I nudged it with my finger. At her smile, I tried to deny her words. Bram Whitlock was me. We were one in the same, weren't we?

"Good, Master." The picture of her swayed the smallest amount. My breath caught as her finger nudged the thin strap of her top off her shoulder. The pale, smooth skin had all my attention glued to the junction of her neck. And lower. Yes, my stare was dropping. I wanted to see more. *To see everything.* "What next, Master? Think. What would Bram do if his Masters were possibly a risk to him, his heir, and the woman he loved? Think," she said more powerfully. "What would Bram do?"

"Kill them," I managed. "I'd fucking kill them all."

Her head slowly shook back and forth. "Bram Whitlock wouldn't be so fast to do that. He's smarter than this Bram. This Bram is blinded by love. He doesn't see. Open his eyes. Focus, and the both of you will be rewarded."

AAMIR

*H*ad I thought the cell I was in before was bad? One guard separated me from possible freedom. At least into the hallways. Now, any plan of escape to save Layla was doomed. I never thought it could get worse than what the guards had called Slave Row. Yet, one act landed me in a place that seemed hopeless to escape. The White Room, as they called this place, was monitored like a federal prison. Not only did I have my cell door to escape, but the one they'd brought me through that cordoned off the hall. Two doors…tons of guards. One I could overpower, maybe even two. Three to four, I didn't stand a chance.

Cursing and pounding continued from the cell next door. I had seen them bring the younger guy in. He'd fought the entire way, and still, he didn't give up. Blood had been smeared across his face and his cheek was slightly bruised from whoever had hit him. It was obvious he hadn't accepted his place here, but I doubted anyone ever could. We were the discarded. The guilty. We'd probably either rot in these cells or be killed by some sort of sentencing. I wasn't naïve to think what I had done would go without some sort of consequence. I was just afraid this wasn't it.

"Open. The fucking. *Door!*"

More banging.

I stared up at the ceiling, wishing I had fight left. A few hours in this room coupled with the reality of what I'd come into had taken its toll. Giving up wasn't there, but my will to needlessly bang for no reason wasn't either.

"Hey! *Hey!*" Bang. *Bang. Bang.* "Let me out of here!"

"Shut up!"

The yell from down the hall had me rolling my eyes and turning to my side, but the demands continued. Minutes passed. When footsteps pounded by, I shot up, straining my ears as a loud bolt sounded and the door to my neighbor creaked opened.

"Do you have a problem, slave?"

Rustling from clothes and multiple scuffling sounds had my pulse soaring. They were wrestling. Hits. Yes, he was getting beat because of his outburst. Voices muffled—more than likely threats with the grunt that followed.

"Now, lay down and shut your mouth. I won't tell you again. If I have to come back, I'll burn out your tongue."

Coughing echoed at the solid connection that was made. He'd been hit again, and given the expelled oxygen, my guess was to his stomach. The bolt returned, and groaning grew with the creaking of his bed.

"You okay, man?"

My clasped fingers tightened against each other as I waited for him to answer my question. A new round of rugged coughs sounded before he sucked in a deep breath.

"Yeah. I think so."

"You can't be doing that. I know you want out—hell, we all do—we just…we have to find another way. Yelling won't do anything but draw attention."

"I shouldn't be here. *I shouldn't fucking be here.*"

"None of us should, but we are. You have to get over that and get your head on straight. It's the only way we have any chance of escaping."

"Escape? Have you seen where we are? There's no escaping this place."

"You're wrong," I snapped. "There has to be a way. I refuse to believe we're trapped in this shithole. If we got in, we can get out."

Time ticked by before the creaking of his bed returned. "Do you have a plan?"

My mouth opened, but my words wouldn't come as the lights flickered and a red glow took its place. Alarms pierced the air, driving my hands to cover my ears. Before I could process what was happening, the bolt on my door drew back and the barrier swung open.

Screams erupted in a chaotic mantra of what I could only assume was panic and excitement. Never in my life had I heard anything so bone-chillingly haunting. It reminded me of a war cry overpowering the exclamations of awaiting victims—of a time no longer lived amongst the normalcy of everyday society. There was hatred in that loud tone. A thirst for the unknown I couldn't begin to understand. Supremacy. Murder. Lust. It was all of those and more. Instinct told me to run—to join in with the pounding footsteps exploding in the hallway. I took a step but jolted to a stop as the neighbor I'd seen earlier burst through my door. He was holding a knife, the blade half the length of my forearm, and there was a wildness in his eyes that didn't match the broken tone he'd had only minutes before.

"What's happening? Did someone break us free?"

"Fuck no," he said, tugging at the door and throwing himself against it to shut us in. "There are weapons everywhere. Looks like population control to me. The prisoners are killing each other. Help me!"

Features tightened as he locked his leg against the wall. The door opened an inch, only to slam back shut against whoever was trying to get in. I didn't wait. I surged forward, putting myself where his leg had been only a split second before. Our feet planted, and we braced our hands on the wall as loud banging reverberated the metal at our backs. There seemed to be more people trying to get in—more force behind the pushing.

"We can't let them get it open. We—" A deep yell broke free as a face as young as mine drew in from exerting so much strength. Fear was there, but also something else. Was it a will to survive? It was all I could imagine as the seconds torturously drew out and the door opened the smallest amount again.

"We're not going to be able to hold it much longer. *They're too strong.*"

Volume from the chants outside rose. Laughter joined in, and me and my fellow slave flew forward at the explosion of weight we were hit with. Managing to get footing, we pushed back, but the door was opened a good few inches. An arm reached through, clawing at my neighbor's gown with blood-drenched fingers.

"Keep holding! Don't…let up."

The order was almost drowned out by the increasing frenzy on the other side. Somehow, they were gaining on us. No matter how hard I tried, I couldn't stop my locked footing from sliding against the cement floor. And they shouldn't have been. Despite the frigid temperature, I was perspiring enough to give me a solid foundation against the weight being applied. It wasn't enough.

A sound pushed through my throat. The man next to me sliced at the arm, but it didn't let go. Blood streaked and soaked into his hospital gown and howling suddenly filled the air. The hair on my arms rose and strength I didn't know I possessed rocketed through, helping me to close the distance on our side. With one hand on the wall and the other in the air, my stare couldn't leave the blade as the slave man next to me thrust down, embedding it into the forearm moving wildly against his stomach. Another howl, this one different and pain-ridden, rang out just behind the door. Fingers seized at his waist, jerking back and disappearing as my neighbor pulled the blade free. And just like that...everything stopped. The door slammed shut and the yells moved farther down the hall. Chaos still reigned, but the attack wasn't focused on us anymore.

"Don't move," the man breathed out. "Keep yourself ready. It may be a test. They may come back."

"I'm not fucking going anywhere."

And I didn't. A million lifetimes could have passed as the minutes stretched on. How many actually did, I would never know. It wasn't until the red glow flickered and the overhead light returned that my neighbor straightened and dropped his leg from the wall. Even then, he kept his back plastered to the door.

"Am I supposed to go back to my cell?"

"Don't leave," I rushed out. "What if it happens again? You can't go. Without each other, we're doomed. They'll kill us. We need to come up with a plan. We have to get out of here."

There was no hesitation as he nodded. Sweat dripped from our faces and a cold like nothing I had ever felt began seeping into my bones. Still, we stood at the door, waiting. Cautious. When clicking automatically tightened and sealed the door, the bolt set. Then, the shots began. *Bang. Bang...Bang...Bang. Bang.*

We threw ourselves at the metal, frozen in terror, confused. I prayed whoever was out there wouldn't try to get inside. For the first time since I had been taken from Athens all those weeks ago, I felt a sense of safety within a cage. My cell was suddenly my salvation, but for how long?

SCOUT 19

ragedy. Life and death situations. Fear. They always pulled people together. The extreme emotions brought on by the realization that life dangled by a delicate thread had a way of warping people's minds to the point of them overlooking the most obvious clues that something wasn't right. I counted on that with Eleven. To merely pray I didn't come off as knowing too much was a risk I couldn't take. He had to believe I was his only hope. That without me, he couldn't make it out of here alive. He needed to trust me. With the events playing out as disturbing as they were, I knew as long as I stuck to pretending to be a slave, he'd bond with me.

Hours had past, and sleep wouldn't come. Not only for me, but for Eleven. It took an extended period of silence to convince him to leave the door. Now, he lay on the mattress as I used his blanket to rest on the floor. The cement was colder than the air biting into my exposed arms and legs. It seeped through the thin material underneath me, causing my entire body to tremble, and Eleven wasn't doing any better. Even on his back, staring up at the ceiling, he shook from the temperature.

"I never got your name."

"Aamir. Yours?"

Dark eyes glanced over, but returned to staring up.

"Dakota...or Nineteen. That's what the guards were calling me. I sort of like it more than my real name. My life was shit. It's always been shit. You'd think I'd be more nostalgic, given the circumstances, but I won't delude myself. I'll take Nineteen over Dakota any day. At least with a new name, I can pretend I can make a new life when we escape. Dakota wouldn't have been able to do that. Dakota was weak. He was trapped in a mundane life with no expectations for any sort of future worth a shit."

Rapidly, Aamir blinked, touching against the gown covering his chest. "They call me Eleven. I hate it."

I didn't push for him to accept who he was. "Then I'll call you Aamir. You can call me Nineteen."

There was no argument or inquiring questions into who I'd been, only silence as he disappeared back into his thoughts. Sleep beckoned, but stayed just out of reach as he began to talk.

"I've been thinking...we won't make it through the main door. There are too many guards. It's locked from the other side and controlled electronically just like these are. If we could find another way..."

His eyes never left that dreaded ceiling as he spoke. It was cement as well. Like a cube of impenetrable force, sealing us in. There was no breaking out of the White Room. Not without help from the outside. I knew this, but I couldn't tell him that.

"Maybe there's another entrance. The hall goes on forever, but it does end. There was no door that I saw. I did notice a hall to the right three quarters of the way down. I don't know where it leads, but I'm not sure we should find out. At least, not yet. If we go out, we may not get back in here alive."

"But if we stay, we're dead anyway. One more person helping those lunatics, and we would have been overtaken." His head turned as he stared at me. "We're screwed no matter how you look at it. Our only chance is to try to break out of here. Can you fight? And I don't mean that as a macho question. It's okay if you can't, but I have to know. *Truthfully*, can you protect yourself?"

Internally, I laughed. On the outside, I let concern show. I knew of this slave's training, but only by chance. Mateo had mentioned it as a warning when he first came into the room. "I think so. I've had some MMA training. A few years. Nothing consistent, but I've never lost a fight."

Eleven's eyes widened as he sat on the edge of the bed. "But you *have* had lessons? You've fought against people?"

"Yeah. I was amateur, but I think I could have gone pro. I was getting pretty good there for a while, but life took over. You can't eat if you don't work."

Full lips pressed into each other as his head nodded in a slow rhythm. For minutes, his hands clasped each other, flattening on his knees, only to go back to wringing as he stayed lost in thought. He did this before when we first left the door. I was beginning to see it was something he did during deep calculation.

"If we're smart, if we move fast, we might stand a chance. We have to see if there's another way out."

"But what if the cell doesn't open again? What if the red light doesn't come back on?"

Worry crinkled his brow. "If they did it once, they'll do it again. It makes no sense for it to be a one-time thing. Besides, these...*prisoners*...they seemed to know what to do. I didn't. I didn't know what was happening, but it was like they were ready. The moment the lights changed, chaos took over. That's not the reaction of confused people. Not to mention, they immediately started running around killing each other. That doesn't just happen. The red light represents something. What, I don't know, but I don't want to find out either. We have to leave. We have to find a way out of here."

My eyes lifted to the tiny window on the door and moved

down to take in the slot below where I knew the food would be distributed. It was good for me to stay close to Eleven, but it was also a risk. The guard who had come in to beat me early left a message. An important one from the Main Master. Staying here would make communication hard, but was there really any other way? I was told to take care of the slave. To protect him until new orders were issued, which were in the works. It would be dangerous to follow Bram Whitlock's orders if we separated. Even more so, if I wasn't fast enough. The red lights were random. What if I was asleep? What if one of Forty-two's followers got to him before I did? I couldn't shake all the questions. This place wasn't safe. If we didn't figure something out, I wouldn't just have to worry about failing my Main Master, I'd lose my life.

"Those gunshots. I think the guards were killing whoever was left out of their rooms. If we do try to find a way out, we can't be caught out there when the lights come back on. We have to search and return as fast as we can. How long would you say the red light was on?"

"Five? Maybe ten minutes? It's hard to say. The entire thing's a blur."

"For me too. Let's say five minutes to be on the safe side. We would have to fight our way through the hall, make it down the other to see if there's an exit, and then back. That's really pushing it. A shit-ton of things could go wrong. We could come back to a room full of those psychos. And that's if we make it back."

"We don't have a choice. We have to risk it."

"Well, we can't right now. All we can do is rest until it happens again. We're going to need our strength."

"But it will happen," Eleven argued. "And when it does, I'm getting a weapon as fast as I can, and I'm finding that hall. You can stay in the room if you'd like, but I really think we stand a better chance if we stay together. Are you with me?"

Before I could answer, voices echoed in the hall. Eleven and I rushed to the small window, taking turns to peek out. Just as I was about to pull back, I saw an all-too familiar face. A face that had my heart racing. And he was coming right for us. Cold, blue eyes locked right to mine, and my breath caught as I stepped back, pulling Eleven with me to stand by the bed.

"What is it? Who is it?"

"Shhh. Just—"

The bolt shot back, and our Main Master didn't wait to throw the heavy door open. Two guards stood just behind him, holding their weapons as they glared in our direction.

"*You.*"

My hand shot to Eleven, fisting the back of his white gown as Bram's eyebrow rose at the slave's anger.

"Would you prefer it be someone else?"

Eleven shifted, relaxing his shoulders as he shook his head. "No. I'd like to get out of here. We both would. Can we go back to the other cells?"

"Slave Row?" The Main Master's head shook. "I'm afraid not. You killed one of my guards. You're lucky I'm not here to take your life."

"I...I couldn't help it. I wasn't in my right mind. I see that now. *Please.* It won't happen again. Just let us go back. We'll be on our best behavior."

"I'm sure you would be, but the board has decided. You're to remain here for the rest of your days, however short lived those may be. It was that, or death by execution. I convinced them you'd enjoy a little more time."

"No. You can't do this! I have no time left if I stay. It's your fault I'm here to begin with. You did this. You brought me here."

"I did, and there's no changing any of it. You'll stay." Blue eyes swept over to me. "I don't believe this is a double occupancy cell. Guards."

"Wait. Wait!" Eleven locked around my arm, pulling me

back as the men surged forward. "Do you know what happens here? Do you know about the red lights? We'll die if you separate us."

"Then you better learn to fight harder. *Learn to survive*, Eleven. That's all you can do at Whitlock."

BRAM

hat I said was the truth in more ways than Eleven knew. The White Room wasn't the only place one had to fight for their life. Corruption ruled at the highest levels. No one knew that more than me. Everleigh's words wouldn't let me forget. Her pleas for the safety of her slave were a reminder that none of us had time if we didn't fight. I needed to fight, and not just to get back the woman I loved. I had to fight for my position as Main Master. Blood may have given me the title, but bloodshed could take it away. Everleigh hinted as much. I knew she didn't trust the men I had placed at the top. Now, I just had to figure out who to keep my eye on, and which ones I could trust.

Eleven's yells came from next door, but I was more focused on Nineteen as I moved in and lowered my voice. He was awaiting instruction. He knew we needed to talk, but what I was about to say wasn't going to sit well with him anymore than it did with me.

"You'll return to him at your first opportunity. I cannot give you good news. As of now, this is where you both will stay."

"But, Main Master."

At the hard jerk of my head, he stopped.

"The board has decided. It's final. Because of Eleven's link with Everleigh, they wanted him dead. I refused to allow that to happen. I am here personally to tell you the verdict. Now..." my voice lowered even more, "if, at some point, the door to the south wing just happens to be unlocked, there are no rules stating a prisoner isn't free. He's to remain in the White Room until death. If he escapes the White Room, well...he's no longer a prisoner, is he?"

"A loophole?"

"One I mean to write in as soon as I leave here. The Whitlock Bible is always in need of new rules and regulations."

"But doesn't the board and High Leader have to sign off on those?"

"Leave that part to me. I was a lawyer, Nineteen. The best damn one money could buy. I know what I'm doing." Stepping back, I kept my face devoid of emotion. There were no parting words for the guards to hear as I left the room. As far as they were concerned, I was returning a slave to his rightful room. Even if they did suspect something, they'd know nothing.

Silence met us at the main door, and I pulled it open as it unlocked. When I walked into the security room, the guards were already standing in respect.

"The slave has been notified. I've separated the two prisoners, but they're free to return to the same cell on the next red light. Is there anything to report to your Main Master?"

The three guards looked at each other and quickly shook their heads.

"No? Nothing?" Their unease was apparent as I took a seat in one of the chairs and crossed my arms over my chest. "Don't hold back," I said, encouragingly. "I know I've been preoccupied lately, but that doesn't mean I'm not your Main Master anymore. You report to your high leader, but I am never more than a question or concern away. You know this, right?"

Two nodded while another's mouth opened, only to close as he joined in.

"Good. How is working under your high leader? Do you believe him fit in his position?"

"Oh, yes. Absolutely," one rushed out.

"What about the two of you? Know there are no consequences for speaking the truth. What is said in this room stays between the four of us."

"Well..." The oldest in the room, a man with dark skin and short hair, shoved his hands in his pockets. He kept his focus on me, refusing to look at the other two guards who were staring at him almost surprised. "I think there're some issues that could be addressed."

"Is that so?" I sat up straighter, glancing at the surname on his shirt. "Please, Makely, continue."

Hesitantly, he glanced to the men. I could tell it was hard for him to go further, but whatever it was had him finally nodding. "It's no secret the guard is divided. First, when...West Harper was in charge with the old ways, and now with your return. Mistress...slave..."

"Everleigh," I supplied.

"As you wish. With Ms. Everleigh gaining guards in her favor, a lot of us are at each other's throats. Some like her. Some don't. Whitlock has been a rollercoaster ride of authority in the last year. I'm not sure the high leader is handling it appropriately."

"What's your overall take of that, Johnson? Where do you stand? What do you believe should be done?"

His lips pursed through his unease. "I stand where I should, Main Master, with whatever you wish. But no one knows the entire story like I do. To choose sides over a situation without having seen it first-hand doesn't accomplish anything. I was one of the main guards detailed to her and West Harper. I was there with Mistress...Ms. Everleigh, through it all. When she was lashed for trying to save a little girl, I watched her refuse to break. She didn't beg her husband to stop. She didn't cry for mercy. I ain't ever seen strength like that. *Ever.* What she did, she did for—" He paused. "I know the slaves play a role here, and I'm not saying anything about what this place is, but that woman was looking out for all involved. To have a place like this run smoothly, there has to be someone who sees all sides. And yeah, she escaped, and that makes her a traitor, but...but...you're trying to bring her back. She left because...well, who wouldn't after all she'd been through? For the high leader to make her out to be some monster is not right. If she's a monster, I'm Santa Claus. I hold no fault to anything she's done. Hell, she killed West Harper. She needs a medal, not a death sentence."

Heat bubbled within at the mere thought of losing her. "Is that what the high leader is insinuating? That Everleigh will be handed a death sentence?"

The guard looked down. "He doesn't say anything particular, but he hints as much."

"What about the two of you?"

Realizing I wasn't going anywhere until I got their opinion, the one who'd somehow put himself behind the man who just spoke, shrugged.

"I didn't know her. Rumors are everywhere—who she was, what she did—I don't know what to think about the situation. My training tells me she's a traitor and I should obey whatever decision my high leader makes."

"And you?"

The third man's face was hard. He didn't like my questioning, that was obvious.

"You want my opinion, Main Master? My real, honest opinion?"

"Absolutely. As honest as you can be."

Two steps forward, and his brown eyes met mine head on. I wasn't sure if he was friend or foe, but I knew one thing for sure:

there was a power in him. *A leader.* The weight of my knife made itself known, but I put my focus on his, analyzing every little tick of his face.

"Whitlock has fallen. Masters come and go. They plot and scheme behind your back. Slaves rise up without fear of the consequences. It never used to be this way. You ran this place with a power few could imagine rivaling, and they wouldn't have dared cross the Main Master. You were feared and admired by all; you just didn't know how much. I wonder, this woman, this slave you love, when she returns, will she fix you, or will she be the end of the Main Master we pray will return for good?"

For seconds, I couldn't speak. Each word weighed against my own self-assessment. Who was Bram Whitlock? Who was he before, and who was he now? Who would he become?

Tapping my finger on the arm of the chair, I let a smile begin to form.

"Thank you for that. Love can do many things to a person. Good. Bad. *Both.* Regardless, let me tell you what it's done for me. Everleigh is the first person I have ever loved. When I say first, I mean that in every sense of the word. She's the only one who has broken through my walls and made me feel. When I feel for something, I don't do it lightly. Hence, the measures I've taken for this search. You can say, after all this time, my eyes are beginning to open. And it's thanks to her. She has made me see what I've neglected to since my return. Whitlock is going through a transition, yes. I won't deny that. I've let you all down, but that's why I'm here talking to you now—something my father would have never done. West Harper wouldn't have either. I care what this place will become. This is my home. This is your home. Whitlock is about to go through some major changes, and they'll be for the better. What I need to know is, if your Main Master returns, the one you say was so admired…will you back me as my guard? Will I have your loyalty no matter my choice of status: single, with a slave, or *married?*"

The older man who'd spoke first looked toward the floor as his smile stretched across his face. "Damn straight you will."

The last hesitated. "Whitlock with the real Bram Whitlock? Yes."

"And you?"

The hard expression still remained as the youngest guard took me in. "I didn't know the old you. I follow my high leader. As far as I know, he's very supportive of you."

"Me, but not my decisions. It'll be something the two of us will have to discuss." I stood, bowing my head, and held the stare of the first man who seemed enthusiastic about my decision to wed Everleigh. I knew he'd caught my hint. *Makely*.

Memorizing his name, I made my departure. The welcoming smile I had kept on my face melted as I stalked back toward the main hall. As much as my mind screamed to video Everleigh so I could see her, I focused more on what she wanted me to do. On what it *meant* to do what she wanted. Did that mean she was above me? Was she giving the orders and I was fulfilling them? I refused to believe that. She was rationality while I was lost. She was light in my darkness. She was greatness and reasoning. And yet, it didn't escape me: her love would start a war.

AAMIR

*S*leep came in mass shades of fresh blood and horrific violence. Everywhere I turned, someone new was coming after me. Weapons at the ready, frozen faces of inhumanity, raced in my direction. There was an emptiness in their wide eyes and open mouths. Crimson already splattered their cheeks, and I didn't miss the hunger in their hunt. It left me frozen in my readied position. Maybe a part of me knew how real this dream could be. Perhaps it was a premonition of what was to come. At some point, I'd face the lions outside my cage. They were ready to eat me alive. My death was their antidote. My life…a release I still didn't quite understand.

I lay in bed, drenched in the aftermath of my nightmare. The *thump-thump* in my chest hit hard. I felt sick, and it had nothing to do with the fact that I didn't eat the food I had been brought hours ago.

"Hey. Nineteen."

My voice came out hoarse. Had I been screaming in my sleep like I had at the end of my dream?

"Yeah. I'm here."

A deep breath came out, and I felt myself relax. I wasn't sure what I would do if Nineteen were suddenly gone. He was all I had. Never had I been close to anyone. It was always me and Layla, but I didn't have her now. A part of me could feel myself latch to Nineteen because of it. I missed that closeness. *I missed my twin.* Just the thought brought tears to my eyes.

"You okay?"

I sniffled. "Yeah. Bad dream."

"It's okay. I'm here. I'm not going anywhere. The moment that red light comes back on, we'll meet up, and fuck them if they try to separate us. It's not going to happen again."

A tear trailed down the side of my face and I nodded, despite that he couldn't see me.

"I've been thinking," Nineteen continued, "when I was coming into your room the first time, all the action was really here in the middle. If we can get by that, we have a good shot of making it to that hall. When you go for a weapon, find the longest one you can. It'll put them at a distance and maybe deter them."

"Okay. I'll see what I can find."

"Also...don't hold back if someone comes after you. Don't be afraid to kill. They're not going to think twice about taking you out. There's no room for hesitation."

"I know." My brow drew in as questions began to emerge. "I never asked how you got here. You said you shouldn't be here. What did you do?"

Nineteen was quiet for so long, I almost wasn't sure he'd heard me.

"I kept attacking the guards."

"But you didn't kill any?"

"Not any of those, no. But I have killed before."

Surprise lit my face. I wasn't sure how I was supposed to feel about that. There was no telling this man's past, but maybe it wasn't what I assumed.

"Who did you kill?"

"It's sort of complicated."

When he didn't elaborate, I stood and began to slowly pace. To push would have been wrong. Nineteen would tell me when he was ready. He wasn't trying to find out more about me, and that was a good thing. I couldn't stomach talking about Greece or the boat ride that followed. *Or Layla.* Especially not her.

Footsteps sounded in the distance followed by a squeaking I knew all too well. Food was coming. *Lunch.*

The guard took his time, and I waited until the knock sounded at my door. I opened the flap and took the tray, pausing at laughter. Lowering, I looked through the gap, nearly dropping my tray as I came face to face with a pair of round, light eyes.

"*Boo.*"

"What…who?" I squinted, not believing what I was seeing as the little girl took a step back. She had long, red hair, braided to her waist. She was wearing the standard white gown, and it wasn't much different in color than her pale skin. Full lips stayed in a big smile, disappearing only long enough for her to sweep her tongue over her bottom lip.

"I saw them bring you in. I like you."

Confused by her demeanor, it was almost impossible for me to talk.

"How did you get out there? They let you pass out the food?"

The appeal she had toward me disappeared. A pout registered for only a second before her face grew tight with anger.

"Did no one teach you manners? You're supposed to ask my name."

"Oh. I'm sorry. What is your name?"

"Forty-two," she said, smiling again. "Yours?"

"Aamir."

"*Wrong.*" The response came out loud and drawn out with aggravation. "Try again."

"Aamir."

"That person is dead. He doesn't exist in here. Again."

"*Aamir*. Only Aamir. Never a number."

Big eyes blinked amid a stoic face.

"I see. A ghost lives amongst us then. I don't like ghosts."

"You don't like me because I won't tell you my number?"

"My daddy always said anyone who has to hide who they are has secrets. Secrets can kill, you know."

"He's Eleven."

At Nineteen's voice, my head whipped toward his cell angrily.

"He's Eleven, and I'm Nineteen. We're new here. Forgive him. He's having a hard time adjusting to our new home. Say, Forty-two, would you mind moving over a little? I'd like to officially meet you, but I can't see you from where you're standing."

The smile was back as she obeyed. Red braids swayed as her head cocked to the side and the smile grew.

"Nineteen. Interesting. How did you get your number?"

"I'm sorry?"

"You're new...right?"

"Brand new."

"Like I said, *interesting*. The count is only up to thirteen. Twenty-seven-thirteen. She was brought in this morning. Dark hair, almost golden eyes, with honey skin. A small woman, not much bigger than myself, although I hear she's a few years older. How are you Nineteen if we're only up two since Eleven's admission?"

Silence.

"I have no idea. I don't make the rules here."

"No. No, you don't," she said, walking more in his direction. "I do. Let me see your number."

The girl disappeared, and the air took on an eerie quiet.

"Just fascinating. You got ink, Nineteen, and it reads as you say."

"Like I said, I don't make the rules. All I know is I'm here."

"How did that come about?"

"Fighting the guards," I cut in. "Forty-two, you mentioned you make the rules. Is that right? I mean, you are out here passing out our food."

Red hair appeared as she came back in my direction. "I said I'm in charge here. Do you doubt me, Eleven?"

My teeth clenched through the name, but I wasn't about to argue with a child.

"No. I don't. I'm just wondering, what are those red lights about? The killing. The chaos. What is the point of them?"

"Fun, of course."

"Fun? Killing is fun for you?"

She sneered. "Hypocrite, I know why you're here. *You sound like Daddy.* Daddy always said it wasn't good to play with dead things. He wasn't saying that anymore when we last had tea. He played the role of a *very* lovely guest. Do you want to know how many cups he made it through before the poison kicked in? I'll give you a hint. The cum was still very much wet between my thighs when he began foaming at the mouth."

I let go of the flap, dropping my tray as laughter exploded from the other side of the door. The cup resting on the top fell to the side, knocking off the plastic lid. Dark liquid I could only assume was tea spilling across the cement floor.

"See you around, Eleven."

Squeaking sounded from the cart, and I ran to the wall dividing me and Nineteen, pounding my fist against it. "Don't drink the tea. Don't drink the tea!"

"I heard. I won't be eating the food either, thank you very much."

A strangled sound left me, and I flattened my palm on my forehead as I made it to the bed to sit. Thoughts and fears spun an anxious cyclone in my mind. We had to get out of here. If I feared the red lights, I now had to be concerned over eating and drinking. Forty-two mentioned she was in charge. As crazy as it sounded, I couldn't deny her status. After all, they'd let her free to deliver the trays. That had to mean something. But was I worrying over nothing? Was the torture extended past the physical into mental? There was no way to know unless I took a chance, which I couldn't risk. It was death by red light or death from poisoning. I wasn't sure which was worse. And the answer didn't come as time ticked by. Hours. Surely night. Even then...nothing.

Sleep took me under enough for the nightmares to rip me awake. I fell back asleep, drifting in and out of lucid, murderous lullabies. I awoke unsure of where I was or if what I'd seen had been real. Reality was slipping. The craziness I had experienced in my cell was returning, and I wasn't sure what it meant. Moans morphed between my sister and the little girl, neither of which I wanted in that way. My brain tried to say it was the trauma of knowing a girl so young had been subjected to such treatment and had turned out the way she was because of it. I didn't know, nor did I want to. I just wished it would stop.

Growling roared from my stomach and I turned on my side, ignoring the hunger that was taking its toll. Nausea kept me awake enough to stay attuned to the surrounding noises, but the darkness from my closed eyes delivered scenes I couldn't control.

Layla was laying with me. We always used to sleep together when we were young. Our parents couldn't separate us, and didn't even try after many failed attempts. I'd hold her, and peace would take over. So badly, I wanted to believe I was really holding her now. I wanted that sensation that everything was going to be alright. The desperation was so strong, I could have sworn the pressure of her back was molded to my chest. My arms would be wrapped around her and that subtle sweetness from the scent of her shampoo would make me feel as if everything were going to be okay.

"You worry too much."

The words filtered through my mind so clearly, she could have really been on my bed for all I knew.

"I'm scared. Layla...I miss you. I promise..."

"You're crying. Don't cry, brother. I'm right here."

"But you're not."

"Well, not yet, but I will be soon. You're going to come get me, Aamir. We'll see each other very soon."

"I don't know how. I'm trapped. I'm not sure I can get out of here."

"You will. In five...four...three...two...

Beep! Beep! Beep!

SCOUT 19

I wasn't ready. Had I missed dinner? Was it the middle of the night? We never got a tray. Time was disorienting me, and the sudden red light was one I hadn't expected. It was too soon after the first. When I pulled guard, they were almost always in the wee-hours of the morning, and usually at least three to four days apart.

Red flooded the walls around me, and my legs were moving so fast as I sprang from the bed, my shoulder crashed into the wall with jarring force. My balance was off, but it didn't stop me from throwing myself into the crowded hallway. Before I could even take in the massacre going on before me, blood sprayed across my face and a man rolled along the side of me as he fell to the ground.

"Take it!"

Aamir's voice boomed as he tossed me a studded club. He was holding something just as long. The morning star had a grip similar to the club, but at the end was a big metal ball with large pyramid-shaped spikes. I wanted to smile at how we'd lucked out, but I didn't have time to do anything but prepare myself as I caught Forty-two's finger pointing right at us. A group of men yelled out, and Aamir and I gave each other a look. There was no time for words. I bolted toward the end of the hall and he was just off to the side of me. Any time someone got close, neither of us hesitated to swing. But we didn't stop. I ran with every ounce of speed I possessed, relieved Aamir was just as fast.

"There! There's the hall!"

The entrance got closer, and so did the men behind us. My pulse skyrocketed and only increased as we turned into the red-glowing hall. It was darker than the main one we'd just left. There was an unease with going into the space. Instinct told me not to go any farther, but the men behind us kept me running. Doors blurred by. I knew they were old cells not in use anymore, but Masters were known to stay in them if the White Room was their cup of tea.

"*Ahhh!*"

Weight crashed into me, and I stumbled, somehow keeping Aamir up as he still attempted to run. He was holding his side, but I saw nothing but blood as he kept his speed.

"You good?"

All he did was grimace and nod as the door ahead grew closer. My eyes kept going between where he was holding and the exit ahead. A slice of dark wetness stained his gown, growing by the second. My hand clamped his bicep, refusing to let go even with how awkward it was.

"You're trapped! You have nowhere to go!"

Ignoring the voice and laugher that followed, I didn't slow our pace, even as we came up on the door. I grabbed the knob, throwing my weight into what felt like a brick wall. Air seized in my chest and Eleven and I crumbled to the floor on top of each other. My mouth shot open and panic hit hard as I fought to find oxygen. It came in another form as pain webbed across my bicep and chest from the whip a man wielded. I inhaled with every-thing I had at the fire burning and tearing through my gown.

"Locked." More laughter from the three of them. They were

all on the younger side, but the man holding the whip had to be close to his fifties, even if he didn't quite appear so. The other two held weapons that could do more damage than shredding the skin. One had a maul, similar to a hammer, but so much bigger at the end, and the last had a cat-o-nine with jagged pieces of metal that could rip us to shreds. "Forty-two says you two aren't very nice. Well…you're to be spared," he said, pointing to me. "But *you*, pretty-boy, you die."

The man's arm reared back, and just when I expected more scorching heat, Eleven and I were tumbling back. The men's eyes grew round like saucers, and shots rang out. In quick succession, the three of them dropped to the ground, limp. Blood oozed from a hole in the center of their foreheads. Snapping my head to the side, I came face-to-face with a pair of black fishnets. The woman stepped back, resting the gun at her side as she smirked at us.

"And here I thought I'd miss all the red light fun. I guess I'm not late after all."

I scrambled to my feet, pulling Eleven up with me. To speak to the gorgeous blonde was almost impossible. Her body was built like an hourglass with luscious curves hugged in a leather business dress. She wore bright red lipstick and dark eyeshadow. It made the blue of her eyes practically glow.

"Surely you have somewhere you should be going? You're not going to block my path all day, are you? There's still time for me to have fun, and you're taking away from that."

"I—right. Thank you…"

"Mistress Jane. And don't mention it." She paused at the door, keeping it propped open. "You're kind of cute. Whenever you decide to stop running, I'll be in my apartment. Two-eighty-three. You come see me, *slave*."

I paused at her all-telling wink. *She knew.* Maybe even knew my real identity. The only way that were possible was if the Main Master filled her in, which I had no doubt.

"Let's go. We have to hurry."

I pulled Eleven toward the closest hall, jolting to a stop at the Mistress's tisks.

"The guard is patrolling down there. Try that hall. It might serve you better."

I obeyed, casting her one more glance before we disappeared around the turn. My mouth was dry, and where I should have been focusing on our escape, the blonde was suddenly taking over my thoughts. Mistress's were new to Whitlock, and in truth, not welcomed. For me, she wasn't going to be an issue. I could get used to having this one around. Especially if she were half the woman she portrayed tonight.

"What the hell was that about? She wanted to kill slaves, but she set us free. That doesn't make sense."

"Are you seriously going to question this? We're free. Plus… she thought I was cute."

I threw Aamir a grin over my shoulder as I slowed at the intersection ahead. I knew there was only one place we could go where we wouldn't be caught but getting there was going to be a chore.

"Do you think she was the one shooting after the red lights?"

"Maybe. I have no idea." I paused, darting my head out to see around the turn. "It's clear. How's your side? Did the whip get you?"

I took in the gaping gown, noting how stupid the question was.

"Yeah. I'm good. He got you worse."

Only then did I notice my own blood-drenched gown. My finger traced over the split skin, and I winced, feeling the depth.

"It's only a cut. Doesn't even need stitches."

"Same here."

"Good. You ready to run for your life? We run, and we go as hard and fast as we can. The hall looks long. There're no guards, but that doesn't mean they're not coming."

"I'm ready."

"You sure?"

"Yeah. Let's get out of here before we're caught."

With one more glance, I burst around the corner, staying true to my words. Training was something I kept on top of and it showed as I began to leave Eleven behind. And I did it for a reason. The more distance I had on him, the better I could survey the dangers ahead. The hall wasn't as big as the one in the White Room. I couldn't fight off a guard with Eleven so close. Not without him possibly getting in the way. That wouldn't fare well for either of us.

Elevation rose, and I knew we were headed in the right direction of the abandoned parts of the fortress. We took a left, then a right. It wasn't until darkness enveloped us that we had made it to the right spot. A large room came into view with sheet-covered sofas and tables. A deep smell of mold filled the air when I stopped to catch my breath.

"What…is this place?"

Deep pants left Eleven as he spun in a slow circle.

"Hell if I know. I was trying to find a way out, but this place is a fucking maze. At least it looks safe."

"Yeah, safe. Let's hope so. I'm not going back to that White Room. I'll die before I go back there."

"That makes both of us."

BRAM

To say I felt more like my old self than ever was putting it lightly. I sipped on my scotch, waiting, smiling at Derek as he remained at the table drinking with me. The meeting had gone smoothly on my part. No one suspected a thing with the multiple new laws passed. At a glance, it appeared as if I were beefing up security. Making everyone safer. There were to be two guards at every post throughout Whitlock, opposed to the one most had before. All Masters would have a lead guard at their beck and call in case a problem arose. That would lift moral and give new leadership to senior guards amongst the flat rank they held now. Slave Row was to become occupied by one slave, versus the double occupancy it held now. With an uprising of the female population, they were growing brave being placed together, causing more problems once bought by their Master. I didn't so much care for that one, but I needed the distraction of more choices. The last was my favorite and the most important. It was in bold, like all titles, so not to be used against me.

Amongst a flight or fight, detainees take the status of current location.

I waited for questions concerning the law. They never came. After dragging out the boring details of the first new laws for hours, everyone just wanted to get it over with. With Torres's never-ending jabber in-between, the members' and Derek's heads were spinning. They blindly signed the papers, ignoring, yet trying to pretend engagement with the narcissistic Master. Torres loved to go on and on about his purchases, about his slave, or what he planned to do with them next. Most times, I cut him off to take care of business, but this time, I didn't stop him; I encouraged him.

"I'm proud of you," Derek said, taking another drink. "I wasn't expecting this from you. You really hit some key areas that I think will be good for Whitlock. I know the guards will be happy with their new promotions. There's been a lot of negativity amongst them lately. They needed this."

"I agree. They deserve a Main Master looking out for them. I plan to start doing that from here on out. They'll be appreciated for the job they do."

"I'll drink to that."

Finishing off his drink, Derek set it down, then opened his mouth to speak. Before he could say a word, his radio went off. It was exactly what I had been waiting for.

"*High Leader, we have a situation down here in the White Room.*"

"A situation?" His hand hovered at his shoulder next to the radio.

"*Yes, sir.*"

His eyes rolled. "Well? *What is it?* You're not calling in with a code red. I have things I need to take care of. Can it not be handled without me?"

"*Two prisoners. They've…escaped.*"

"What? Escaped how?"

I grabbed my glass, smiling as I headed over and poured another drink.

"Mistress Jane, sir. She was coming in through the south door like she's been granted when she was ambushed. She did shoot three we assume tried escaping as well, but...two got out. I tried to pull up the tape to see for myself, but it's all distorted."

I froze, my smile growing. *Everleigh.*

"Shit! Give me a few minutes. I'll start the search."

"Search?" I turned, taking a bigger drink. "I'm afraid that's not necessary in the way you intend."

"Excuse me?"

I shrugged. "According to the fight or flight law you just signed off on, it would seem they're no longer prisoners. Or...*detainees.* They're slaves again. If you want to do your search, it'll be to return them to Slave Row. Not the White Room."

Derek didn't move as he stared at me with a mix of anger and disbelief. He clicked the button, growling his question. "What slaves escaped?"

"Uh...twenty-seven-eleven, and...twenty-seven-nineteen."

"You! This is your doing. You're doing this for *her.*"

"I don't know what you mean."

"You're lying. Everleigh Harper wanted that slave, and you mean to give it to her. A traitor to Whitlock! An outlaw and disgrace to this place!"

My glass hit the table with a hard clunk, and I took two steps, narrowing my eyes as I put myself inches from his face.

"I'm only going to tell you this once. I put my trust in you for all things Whitlock. I considered you the closest thing to a friend I've allowed myself to have. I've *allowed* you to keep this position. In a breath's time, all of that could come crashing to an end. If you ever, and I mean *ever*, call her a traitor or anything resembling it again, I won't just dispose of you as my high leader. I'll make it so you never speak another word again. Are we clear?"

"You're not in your right mind."

"I've never been more myself than I am right now."

"You're wrong. I knew you before she went back to being a free slave. I knew you, Bram. This isn't you."

"I know where you're going with this and know I'm a step ahead of you. This is me in love. This is me. *Me*. You have no right to say it's not. You never saw me in love, nor do you have the evidence to say you have. You question my mind; I have guards who question your leadership."

"That doesn't matter. There's only one thing that does. Whose side do you think the board will choose if it came down to my way—the Whitlock way—or Bram's way—the Everleigh way? Who will they choose, me or you? Whitlock, or Everleigh's Whitlock? Better think twice before you threaten me again. I've always been on your side, but once you cross the line, I choose Whitlock. That's my job. That's who I am, and that's what I'm meant for."

I didn't go after Derek as he turned and left the room. My teeth ground into each other, and it took everything I had not to go slit his throat for speaking about Everleigh that way. If I didn't need him, I would have. As it were, Derek played a vital role for what I envisioned for the future.

Ringing had me taking a deep breath and pulling out my phone. I hit the video button, glad Everleigh decided to show me her face. I needed to see her. I needed her more than ever.

"You did it."

She was smiling and had more of a glow than she had in the previous call. Her health was returning, which helped calm the concern over her wellbeing.

"I told you I would."

"Not exactly, but I knew you'd take care of it. Thank you."

"No, *thank you*. You distorted the tape. You gave me the motivation I needed to make the changes. I've been watching the footage on the Masters. Very interesting lives they lead. Was there something in particular you wanted me to see? If so, I still haven't run across anything substantial."

"Keep watching."

"Okay..." I took in the pale blue blouse she was wearing, raking my eyes over the material. "Do I get rewarded for my good deeds?"

A laugh filled the room, and I couldn't help but smile.

"You'd like that."

"Of course I would. As it is, if I'm going to get to see you naked, I'd prefer to be in bed."

"And what would my Master be doing while watching me? Would you stroke your cock and imagine it being deep inside me? Can you feel me around you right now?"

Heat engulfed my face racing down my body as my cock hardened. I gave my tie a hard jerk, moving to reach over and down my drink.

"You're a naughty slave. You're lucky you're not here. I'd put you over my knee for trying to work me up. But yes. Fuck yes. Unbutton your shirt. Let me see what's mine."

No hesitation. One of Everleigh's eyebrows lifted and the mischievous grin she had on her face stayed in place as she propped the phone up on the table she was sitting at and slowly worked the buttons free with her good hand. Pale skin became exposed, revealing cleavage that made me hold my breath. She pushed her shirt over one of her shoulders and made a path down her chest with the tips of her fingers. When she met the lace covering one of her breasts, she peeled it back, tracing around her nipple.

"Jesus. Fuck. *Slave...*"

The unspoken plea in that one word had my heart aching. To touch her, to taste her, and have her as mine again came with the all-too suffocating feeling. Everleigh was in my blood. In my being. She'd taken me over long ago, and with time, her potency was death. In her own way, she'd killed Bram Whitlock. He belonged to her more than himself. He always would.

"Is this what you wanted? You want me?"

"More than anything."

Squeezing against the hard nub, she bit her lip, letting out the most intoxicating moan. My lips parted, and I squeezed the phone, bringing it closer.

"Meet me somewhere. Right now. Me and you. No one else on my side. You have my word. I want to see you. I *need* to see you."

Everleigh's heavily lidded eyes opened more at my words. The lace was suddenly returned, and she grabbed the phone, composing herself.

"It's not time."

"Love doesn't operate off a clock, slave. Meet me. All I want is one night. That's all I'm asking for."

"It's too risky. They'll be watching your every move after tonight."

"There has to be a way for us to see each other."

Multiple expressions flashed over her face while I watched her scheme. It was fascinating and terrifying at the same time. The way her mind worked amazed me. She was always in control. Always a step ahead.

"If you want to see me, you must do exactly as I say. Do not cut corners because it is convenient or change any part of my plan because you think there's a better way. You say love doesn't operate off a clock. You're right, but where love is spontaneous, it is also patient. Can you wait for me, Master? No matter how long or short it may take?"

My pulse was in my throat as I nodded. "I'll wait forever if I know there's a chance to see you again."

"Then, let us plan."

SCOUT 19

*L*ights snores came from the opposite side of the closet —soft…slow. I'd been sitting in the dark for hours, waiting for Aamir to fall asleep. My chest ached, and my mind swam with what I was supposed to do. The Main Master hadn't given me instruction on anything other than escaping the White Room. Did he know I'd come here? Was I supposed to go to him with the slave? I had to figure out a way to communicate without having it blow up in our faces. But how? I couldn't go to his place. I needed a phone. A Whitlock phone, and there was only one way to get one of those. I needed to take it from a guard or scout. My best bet was doing that now that Eleven was asleep. The sooner I got that out of the way, the better.

Lifting as quietly as I could, I pushed open the cracked door of the abandoned apartment and made my way to the entrance. A creak had me pausing while I listened for movement from Eleven. When all remained quiet, I opened it even more, peeking my head out. It was still dark, but it wouldn't be for long. Morning was coming, and with it, the danger would increase. It was vital I find a phone, and fast.

Jogging as fast as I could, I made it back to the empty lobby. I knew if we took the hall we came in at, I'd have to go farther to find guards. My eyes went over to the back opening, and I entered the pitch-black hall with trepidation. Warnings blasted in my mind, but I continued at a steady pace until the glow from the adjoining hall came into view. It didn't take long before easing into the light that I heard voices. Not one, but two.

"Better, right? This will make time fly by. Tell me more about that game?"

"It's badass. The graphics are just amazing. You should stop by after the shift and check it out."

"After the shift?" A laugh. *"We'll be lucky not to get put on the search. I bet those Masters are pissed at being woken up."*

"Better than dead if those slaves get to them first. At least this way they'll have some sort of warning."

Tiptoeing, I got closer to where the hall intersected with two others. The edge of the guard's pants were visible and one step or turn, I'd be caught. There was nowhere to hide in the light, and it was dim enough, he'd see me.

"Do you buy the Mistress's story?"

"What do you mean?"

The guard hesitated with his response, shifting on his feet. The phone flashed on his belt, and I held my breath as I got closer. I needed to unclip it, but how I was going to remove it from his belt, I wasn't sure.

"She shot three times. Killed three wackos. Yet, two got free. She had plenty of bullets left in there to put them down, but she didn't. Now, with this new law about prisoners becoming slaves again if they escape? If you ask me, the Main Master wanted those two to escape, and that woman helped him."

Loud laughter. *"Don't be ridiculous. She killed three and had a moment of morality. She's a woman—"*

"Not just a woman, a Mistress."

"That could mean anything," the other argued. *"Maybe she's*

into weird shit. That doesn't make her a killer. She froze and couldn't kill any more and they escaped."

"Maybe, but I don't know. You can't say that shit isn't suspicious."

"Suspicious, yeah. Condemning, no way. Worst case scenario, the bitch was probably worried about breaking one of those expensive nails. You know how women are."

Both laughed, and I suppressed the anger that flared at their stupidity. The woman was a hell of a shot. Remorse? Fuck no. She didn't have a drop of guilt over what she'd done. If anything, she probably enjoyed it.

One of the guards yawned, and I eased my hand forward, hovering over the phone attached to his belt. It wasn't the kind the scouts carried, but more of the older style, one-length, blocky cells. They resembled more of a walkie-talkie than phone but definitely had more capabilities than the ones the scouts used.

"Fuck, I'm hungry."

The scout dropped his weight against the wall for support, and I jerked my hand back. When he didn't immediately rise, I let myself move back over the phone. Pressing my lips together, I grabbed the top, squeezing the clip. Breaths wouldn't come. My pulse hammered so hard my hand began to shake. Gently, I lifted, keeping the clip as open as I could. Just as I brought it up and disconnected it, the guard rocked to the side, facing away from me. Immediately, I drew the phone to my chest, racing as lightly as I could back to the dark. And I didn't stop until I was running down the hall to our room. The moment I got inside, I shut the door, feeling my legs shake from the adrenaline. Even after all the scout missions, nothing had affected me as much as this. My Main Master's orders were riding on me. I had no room for error. Not a single one.

Illumination from the phone lit up my chest as I walked to the closet, turning the screen enough to catch a glimpse of Eleven curled in the corner. He was still out cold. Relief hit even more as I made my way to the edge of the mattress. Seconds went by as I searched through the different icons, finally making it into the settings. Rerouting the phone to use my number was easy enough. Whitlock phones were all linked and connected, and I needed to make sure this one didn't ring if the guard tried to call it.

Nineteen: Held up in an abandoned apartment. Any news from the Main Master?

Mateo: Negative, Nineteen.

My mouth parted in surprise.

Nineteen: He's told you nothing?

Mateo: Not a thing. Wherever you are, stay until I get word. They're pulling patrols, but I'll try to get word out amongst the guard to stay out of the rooms. No promises.

Nineteen: 10-4. I'm going to need supplies. The slave is asleep. Can you get someone up here to bring me some things?

Mateo: I'll see what I can do. Where can we meet you?

Standing, I glanced out the windows and counted the floors.

Nineteen: Fourth floor lobby.

Mateo: Be there in fifteen.

It hardly took any time to slip out of the room and make my way to the end of the hall. I stayed in the darkness until I saw a tall silhouette enter the room. Mateo stopped in the middle, and I headed out to meet him. He towered over me as I got closer, and immediately tossed two uniforms at my chest. They were standard wear by Whitlock guards: black cargo pants, black belt with a matching black t-shirt. He held two pair of boots in his other hand and placed them on the top of the pile I held.

"Clothes is all you get. You want food or water, you'll have to get it from City Center. There's no way I could get away with bringing all that up here without it looking obvious. Dressed in those, you shouldn't have a problem. Keep your head down regardless."

"When do you plan to write the Main Master? I can't stay here long."

"No, you can't. I can tell the guard whatever I want, but you know they take orders from the high leader. If he's present, they will check every inch of those rooms."

"I know. That's what I'm worried about."

"I've already written him, but he's probably asleep. I'll let you know when I hear back."

"Thanks."

"You bet. Now, go, and keep quiet in there. Don't head to City Center until after daybreak. It'll be less likely anyone important will be paying attention then."

I nodded, walking backwards as he headed for the hall. The moment I made it through our door, I could feel the energy inside change. I barely ducked before a broken table leg whizzed by where my head had been.

"*Fuck, Aamir.* It's me."

Wild eyes were barely visible in the darkness.

"You scared the shit out of me. Where did you go? Where did you get all that?"

Voices in the distance had me grabbing his arm and pulling him back to the closet. Deep breaths came from us both. Had Mateo stirred suspicion? Did they know where we were?

"Put these on. I was looking for food and water when I came across a room full of old uniforms. We won't stand out as much, but we have to be quiet. They're searching for us, and they're close."

"Shit." The clothes and boots were pulled from my arms, and I listened to the voices grow louder as I got dressed too. There were some bangs here and there, but surprisingly, they passed without coming inside.

"What do we do? Where do we go now?"

"I don't know. I think we need to stay in place for a while.

Let them drop their guard so we can make it out without too much of a fight. Plus, we need a plan."

"Right. I'm sorry. I just want to get the hell out of here."

"Don't apologize," I said, lowly. "I know what you mean. I want out too."

"This doesn't seem real. None of this does. I mean...I killed a man. Yeah, he was a guard here, but he was still a person."

I opened the door, allowing the smallest amount of light to break through. Eleven's face was drawn in and I could see his dilemma. The first kill was the one you always remembered. For some, it was the hardest to stomach. But something told me the slave would kill again before this was over. Maybe even a lot.

"Slave Row was really no different than the White Room. It's the color. The walls. It does things to some. It messes with their minds. That's probably what it was."

"Maybe." He grew quiet, pausing. "I don't feel bad about taking that man's life. I know I should, but I don't, and that's what's bothering me. I don't fear murder. A part of me almost seems to need it. Ever since I was taken, since my twin Layla and I were taken, killing has been the only thing on my mind. I thought it was because of the protectiveness in me, and maybe it is, but I failed to keep her safe. Maybe I missed opportunities of killing someone that could have freed us. I keep going over everything, but it's pointless. I failed her, and I lost her. I have to get out and make this right."

"Maybe you will. We got this far."

Eleven grew quiet, eventually lowering to sit against the wall. I joined him, putting my attention on the random patrols that came and went. Hours passed, and our stomachs growling were the only sounds between us. He didn't feel the need to talk, and I wasn't naturally much of a talker to begin with. More time, and I let myself doze off and on. The snores came from next to me once again, and I let it take me under even more. Vivid colors appeared—shades of blue, black, with hints of white. A room. My grandfather's room here at Whitlock. As far as I knew, it was still empty. And would remain so until our lineage ended. After all, it was bought and paid for. I considered moving into it at times but would have been a laughing stock for who I was. I wasn't him. I didn't have money like everyone assumed he'd had. But I would soon. At least enough to get set up in there. If I could finish out this mission for the Main Master, I'd be established with not just a dream job at Bram Whitlock's side, but at my rightful, respected place amongst the Masters' apartments. I could even be a Master if I wanted. Mistress Jane popped into my head, and I held to the vision, basking in her curves and red lips. That was a possibility. Me a Master; her a Mistress. I liked that.

"I haven't heard anyone for a while. Is there a bathroom here?"

Colors melted, and I groaned as I became aware of the bright light breaking through the crack in the door.

"I think I came across one last night. Opposite side of the room."

Eleven stood and I waited until his footsteps grew farther away before I took out the phone and checked the time. It was almost nine. I'd slept so much longer than I'd thought. No messages came up, so I stuffed the phone back in my pocket. Standing brought the throb back between my chest, and I placed my palm against it as I headed into the room. It was smaller than the standard apartment for the Masters. It looked more like a hotel room versus the living area and kitchens they had now.

"Fuck, I'm starving. Do we have a plan?"

I stopped at the mirror, lifting my shirt to see the lash across my chest. It hadn't bled anywhere near as much as Eleven's had, but both our wounds had stopped bleeding hours before. I turned, heading to the window, not turning back to look at Eleven as he closed in behind me. For being early in the day, the only ones below seemed to be a handful of slaves. The Masters were either away dealing with their real lives or still sleeping.

"There's food down there. There has to be," I said, covering my tracks. "I'll go see. You stay up here."

"No way. I'm not letting you go alone."

I spun, throwing him a look. "I don't have a sister on the outside who needs rescuing, you do. If anything happens, you can still try to make it out."

"We can wait for food."

"Don't be absurd. We have to eat and drink, or we'll get too weak. I'll be fine."

Confliction registered, but he ultimately nodded.

"I won't be long. Stay in this room no matter what. If you hear anything, go to the closet."

"Okay. Be careful."

"Always."

Heading to the door, I opened it, then paused as I looked both ways. *Clear.* I pulled the door closed behind me and jogged back toward the lobby. When I approached, I jolted to a stop at the sound of whispering voices. They continued, and I moved in closer to hear what they were saying.

"My sources are not wrong. He knows nothing."

"You're positive? Because if he suspects—"

"You question my intelligence? I'm the fucking CIA director. I know everything that happens on the inside and out. Bram Whitlock believes what I tell him. As we speak, he's going over my report on Everleigh Harper. I've got eyes out there that say she's possibly held up on a yacht just off the island of Crete. Does he know that? No, he does not. He thinks she's recovering in Sicily, and he'll continue to believe so because I'll leave him no choice. Everleigh Harper will not be found alive. She is a risk to Whitlock and everyone here, just like you said. Sending that scout after her was the smartest thing you've ever come up with, Barclane. Have you heard anything from him?"

There was a pause, and I lowered as I waited.

"Not since he came to see me a few days ago. I have plans to call him later and get a report. He had to clear it with Mateo and Bram, and he managed to do just that. I'm not even sure where they sent him. I didn't ask for fear it would bring suspicion. But he's waiting on my call. Thanks to you, now I can make it. A yacht off Crete. Sounds like a good place to die."

"You make sure your guy doesn't screw this up. Mine are waiting in the wings, but it's dangerous for me to send them in. Her people would attack, and we can't risk it. We need this...Nineteen to take the blame for her murder. It'll make more sense that way. No one would question a rogue scout directly from Whitlock. If we can capture the act on film as evidence, even better."

"Film? How would we do that?"

"Body cams. My men have to wear them to account for their whereabouts on a mission. At least these missions. Main Master's orders. He doesn't trust them, and for good reason."

"Right. Well, Nineteen will do as I tell him."

"He better. I'm not letting some conniving cunt rule at our Main Master's side. I saw her work over Master Harper. She's dangerous."

"You have no idea," Master Barclane growled. *"It'll be my pleasure to see her dead. And when it happens, we celebrate."*

"Done."

The other Master nodded, and I kept still as they headed in different directions. My fists were so tightly clenched, I could barely force them open to grab my phone. Use me? Set me up? They had no idea who they were messing with. It was time I took matters into my own hands and contacted the one person who would make them regret the day they ever turned against him.

BRAM

To rule was to regulate. I used to think my father had it figured out, but had he? It was true he'd thwarted attempts on his life, and yes, he'd taken out Masters for their disloyalty. But I couldn't remember there being so much scheming during his reign.

I tossed and turned, trying to ignore the latest news of betrayal and how each hour of the day and night dragged on into an endless obsession between work and following the plan Everleigh had laid out for me. I was meticulous with each detail, triple checking and viewing it from every angle so nothing could go wrong. Mixed in the middle between knowing someday she'd come to me to keeping a close eye on the Masters, I saw her in the way she last appeared before we had hung up. Happy eyes, that smile—a devilish, mischievous smirk on those pouty lips. The combination drove me wild. Her entire demeanor wrapped itself around me in a web I couldn't escape. In one I didn't want to. It lured in my Master: the real Bram Whitlock. She may have appeared to hold the cards now, but I knew ways to wash that look off her face and have her moaning and begging me instead, and I planned to make it happen. The tables had turned—they always did. Before it was over, Everleigh would be back to being my slave. Maybe not in the ways she once could have been, but I was the Master. Her true Master, and she knew that. *She needed it.*

A yawn came as I carried my glass of water into my bedroom and headed to the adjoining restroom. It was morning and I had yet to go to sleep. My eyes were heavy as I rushed through my shower routine in a daze. Our conversation repeated on a loop, but I didn't hear her words or our plan. It was her face. That beautiful face that flashed multiple expressions of anticipation. It told me although she spoke of time, it might not be months or years before we saw each other again. It gave me hope. Something I probably shouldn't have had, but I couldn't help it. Maybe it was this obsessive love. Maybe I was a fool.

Pink darted out as she'd licked her lips. She'd done that a lot when I began teasing her as she'd teased me. Our eye contact through the video never wavered. Not for long. We were in tune. We were one. Again, the tongue. *Her lips.*

Whether I moaned as I got out of the shower, I wasn't sure. I dried off, then slipped on my pajama bottoms before climbing into bed. I took a big drink of water and lay back, closing my eyes. Everleigh met me in the darkness like I knew she would. My body tingled, and I felt giddy for the first time in as long as I could remember. She'd be back soon. I could feel it. *Feel her.* And then we'd be together again. Even if it wasn't on the terms I wanted, I didn't care. Hell...whatever she wanted, she could have. I needed her no matter what that meant. I needed...*God, if I could only think.* Her plan came back through and with it, a moment of clarity. She had wanted me to open Whitlock to her in two different ways, and I had. Was it a trap? A scheme I was overlooking because of my love for her? I wouldn't think of that. My heart...it wouldn't let me. Somewhere deep inside, I could feel the depth of how connected we were. Depth. Heavy. Yes, I was so heavy.

Warmth poured from my skin and the tingling exploded under what I could have sworn were fingers trailing up my forearms. I did moan then. My cock hardened painfully and clicking pinched my wrists, pulling me out of my half-dream state. Snapping my eyes open, I couldn't stop the almost painful beating of my heart. I tried to jerk my body at the internal alarms, but nothing moved but a twitch of my finger.

"Shhh. Don't worry. I didn't give you much. Not nearly as much as you gave me in my drink."

"Ever...leigh?"

The name slurred from my tongue and felt so foreign. I almost wasn't sure I had said it at all. Was I still dreaming? Was this real? She looked the same as she had on the phone. Well, minus the dark clothes and makeup she was now wearing. She looked like heaven amid the hell surrounding her.

"You're...here? This is r-real?"

She laughed, pulling up the tight black dress to straddle me. Slowly, she lowered her chest to mine. We were inches apart. The smell of her perfume hit me hard, and I somehow found the strength to grind my cock against her lower stomach.

"You have a special gift for me. I've come to collect. My slave is not safe here without me. I couldn't very well take him and leave without giving you a present in return. You've done so much to keep him safe. That wouldn't be a very nice thing to do, Master." Fingers traced across my cheek, toward my mouth, and my body couldn't stop from reacting on its own. She had drugged me. But, how?

The water by my bed. Shit.

The purr was cut off as her lips crushed into mine. The joining was so real and electrifying, my heels were digging into the mattress. I was doing everything I could to feel more of her. To get us closer.

Everleigh's tongue swept into my mouth and we both moaned. The moment I tasted her, I knew this was real. Memories barreled through—us together. Passion. Ecstasy. *Love.* She was in my bed, even if I knew it wasn't going to be for very long.

"I always loved when you slept. Your face is so peaceful. No hard lines or angry expressions. You're beautiful, Bram Whitlock."

Again, she made it impossible to speak with her kiss. Not that I cared. I drank her in just as hard as I had hit the bottle of scotch since her escape. I wanted to be drunk off her. To know nothing but Everleigh in our moment.

"Take." Deep pants left me as I used my strength to move my arms. "Take these off. I want...to touch you. I have—"

"You want my trust? You want me to eventually come back? Give this to me. Show me I can come and go at my own free will without you intervening in any way. If you can, I promise when I finish everything, you will have me. All of me, just the way you want."

"I took my men...out of the field...*for you.* No one...will see that you come."

"I know. I was told the moment you did. They think you've lost your mind, Master. They think you've gone crazy with love. Have you?" Her hand slid down my bare side and stopped where my silk pajama bottoms rested on my hip. Still, I couldn't stop from moving my cock against her stomach. If she didn't stop, I wasn't going to make it to this gift she wanted to give. My body was oversensitive. Every touch radiated through parts of me I didn't even know existed.

"Yes. God...yes."

"Tell me you love me."

"I love...you. I love you. *I love you.*"

Each exclamation was more forceful than the last. The lining of my pants was lifted, and a growl mixed with a moan rumbled through my being. Lifting the smallest amount, she wrapped her hand around the length. Pre-cum smoothed over the head as she stroked up, and she used the slickness to slide down to begin a slow, torturous rhythm. Clinking erupted from the headboard. I knew I was moving. Hell, my entire body was under her control.

"I love you too. Do you want me to show you how much?"

Tighter, she clutched around my thickness through the thrusts. A desperate sound left me. A begging. A plea like nothing I'd ever given her.

"Please, slave. Show me. Kiss...me."

The beginning of a smile appeared as her chest separated from mine. She was getting farther away. Closer to where I wanted. Angling, she gave me a view of her profile. Her ass was in the air and her lips were suddenly encasing over the pajamas covering my cock. All I could do was stare down with my mouth slightly open in awe.

"I think about tasting you all the time."

Turning to look at me, her tongue darted out to flick over the material. Shocked at her behavior, at the innocence that was gone, played an evil game over my mind. Half of me wanted to flip her over and spank her ass for being so bold. The other half was frenzied to the point of cutting off my own hands to tackle her down so I could have her *my* way.

"I'm yours. Every single...part of me. Do it, slave. Fuck. Do. It."

My pants were peeled to my thighs, and for what felt like forever, Everleigh didn't move as she stared at my length. Continuously, she licked her lips, watching me. I could see her hunger, and it rivaled mine.

"I forgot how big you are. I need..." She swallowed, lowering to grip around me once more. She didn't even seem to care to continue to speak. Her tongue came out and flattened, circling my head before she opened wide, taking me in. Heat singed over my skin and my hips somehow arched at the unbearable pleasure. The paralysis part of the drug was wearing off. I knew I only had a few more minutes and I'd have more control. But could I hold off that long? She was taking me deeper—so fucking deep—and stroking my length as her lips met her hand. The suction she applied was killing me.

"You have to...slow down."

Vibrations from her moans left my heels digging back into the bed.

"Everleigh. *Slave.*"

The pop that followed the break of suction traveled deep into my balls. My breath caught, and I turned my head through the battle I waged inside. The revelation had me moving back to face her. Back and forth, I put my attention on the fact that I was doing something on my own.

"Take these damn things...off. You can trust me. I won't detain you after we're finished. We made a...deal."

Talking in complete sentences was as hard as walking around shitfaced. It took all my concentration, but I was almost there. Everleigh's hand stopped and her eyes went right to mine.

"Take. Them. Off."

The domination was exactly what I knew she needed. Her slave was never so clear to me than in that moment. She lifted, blinking rapid through her thoughts. Just when I thought she wasn't going to obey, she reached toward the table and grabbed the key. In suspicious glances, she watched me as she unlocked the cuffs and eased my hands to the bed. I flexed my fingers, but still couldn't lift my arms.

"Now, take those clothes off and let me taste you."

"I should have given you more of the drug."

Grabbing the hem of her dress, she slowly maneuvered the dress over her head and let it drop to the bed. A bandage covered her shoulder and she winced as her arm lowered. She was wearing a black lace bra and panties. A matching garter rested at her hips, holding up black stockings. Reaching down, she began to unbuckle the strap on her heels. I shook my head, not taking my gaze from hers.

"Leave the shoes. Lose the panties and bra. Then, come put your pussy on my mouth."

The shiver that raced down her body had me fighting the drug. I flexed my fingers again, barely able to lift my hand before it collapsed. Everleigh obeyed, rising to her knees as she made her way to my chest. There was no embarrassment in her advance. She reached forward, clutching my hair as she separated her legs and put one over each shoulder. With her position, I knew all she could see was my eyes, and I loved it.

The tip of my tongue traced her folds, pushing between them to dip into her entrance. Flavor burst over my senses, intoxicating me with nothing but her. *Just like I remembered*—like I dreamed a million times since her escape. Fisting my hair tighter, she began to rotate her hips. Wetness flourished, and so did every part of me. Holding the headboard, she angled forward, letting me sweep over her clit. The tremor that shook her wasn't enough. She repeated the action, torturing herself by letting me flick over the sensitive nub even faster. When I added suction, she let out a loud cry and threw her head back. But she never stopped moving. She was a goddess of Whitlock's making. Of evil and power combined with the woman she was meant to be. The realization was like ice water in my veins. I had clung to the memories of the old her, but in truth, it was *this* version that drove me to the point of no return. She was meant for a man like me. A man of power. A man who needed a firm hand and a reality check. I'd been trying to figure out who I was, and Everleigh was right here showing me everything I needed to know.

From nowhere, my hands flew to her thighs, squeezing with so much strength, I swore I'd brand my fingerprints on what was mine forever. A gasp sounded, and she jumped, staring back down at me. Lightly, I sunk my teeth into her fold, tugging gently as I gave one more suck and broke away, smiling. It wasn't a nice smile. It wasn't dark. Evil. It was one of immeasurable ownership reserved just for her.

"I can't believe you came so soon. You had to have left the moment we got off the phone. You do trust me."

"Yes…and no. I'm trying."

"Thank you." I paused, almost afraid to ask my next question. "Tell me you're not leaving the moment we finish." I used my grip to ease her pussy to my chest, aggravated when I didn't have the strength to go any further. Everleigh seemed to notice and laughed. She scooted down to the tip of my cock, letting her chest rest against mine again.

"I'll stay as long as I can. We'll see how it goes."

"Then we're not stopping. I'll keep going until you're too weak to walk. And then I'll go again."

"I'm holding you to that. If I can walk fine when I leave here, I'm never coming back. Make me sore. Give me something to remember you by."

"Oh, baby, you're in trouble. Shut that sweet little mouth of yours and kiss me. Don't stop kissing me until I say."

Her tongue plunged into my mouth and flashes from the past blinded me. Once, I had let her have control of kissing me. I hadn't kissed her back. Not immediately. How I had ever held off for as long as I had, I'd never know. We were so different now. *Both of us.* But different in a good way. At least I hoped. Our plan had a chance of backfiring. I could lose everything, including her. I didn't like it, but what choice did I have if I wanted a life with her willingly at my side?

Hot wetness encircled me, and we both broke apart, inhaling deeply as her channel stretched around me. Inch by torturous inch, her pussy clutched me like a vice. No amount of wetness made it easier. Withdrawing, I thrust enough to have her nails tearing into my shoulders. The sting was magnified by the drug, warped with pleasure and pain. Blood tickled over my skin as it made a path to the bed. My brain zeroed in on it and I stiffened through my own demons. I had killed slave girls for touching me while I was beating and fucking them. Hell, I had killed them just to see the life leave their eyes. She didn't know those secrets. Not the details anyway. Blood fueled me. It fed the monster inside. Everleigh had seen that first-hand when she was a slave. But I was different now...wasn't I?

A cry filled the room, and I felt my hands lock on her hips as she sank down my entire length. She was still riding me, still taken over by the desire blinding her from my potential danger. All I could think about was the blood. It was there. I couldn't get rid of it. To deny what fueled my twistedness was pointless.

"Slave." I swallowed hard, squeezing my eyes shut. "Everleigh."

"What is it?"

She was leaning down against me now, grinding her hips as she kept her hypnotic pace. I managed to bring my hand up and sweep my fingers over the small wound she'd given me. Red masked my fingertips, and before I could wipe it free and explain, she grabbed my wrist, rubbing the crimson over one cheek, and then the other.

"War paint. Fitting, isn't it?"

Everleigh was flipped onto her back so fast, she squealed in surprise. Adrenaline raced, bringing my body back to life as I fucked her mercilessly. Her face, the blood, it was fantasy over-load. Full lips were parted through the loud moans and her lids were so low, her eyes were barely open. One of my arms collapsed to my elbow, but I didn't stop pounding into her pussy. I couldn't. Not even when she screamed out from release and spasms shook her. War. Yes. We were in so many wars. *Her and me. Her and Whitlock. Me and my members. Me and the high leader. Us and our demons.* It was never-ending—and that was the truth.

My hand locked around her throat as I lowered my lips to hers. The hold was nothing more than a claim of my ownership. I kept it there as my cum shot deep. In these moments, I was on top. *I was in control.* I was the Master and she was my mouse, and the short time we had together was only beginning.

AAMIR

ow long had I been waiting? An hour? Two? Three? Panic that something happened to Nineteen left me pacing the small length of the room. For a long time, I had kept my gaze on the grassy area below, waiting to see him head to the stores, but he never did. At least not while I was watching. Or maybe I'd missed him? It was a large area and the crowd was getting thicker as time went on.

"What do I do? What do I do?"

I kept trying to get my brain to work. Nothing would come. We agreed me staying in the room would be best. Layla needed me. But I didn't even know where to go to leave this place. What if I made a wrong turn? What if I got caught by the guards? Surely they would recognize me?

My head was fuzzy as I lunged back toward the window. Men in suits, some in jeans, walked around closer to the stores. Others were in long dresses and head-wraps. It was impossible to see who they were, but I knew they had to be the slaves. Nothing looked out of sorts. No one appeared fearful or watchful of a scene going on around them.

A sigh left me, and I turned, glancing at the door. Loyalty

said I couldn't just stay here if he was in trouble. Not knowing if he was was the hardest part. It had me arguing with myself on what the right thing to do was. Wouldn't he come for me if he thought I was in danger? My mind said yes, but what if I left and made things worse? I had to stay a little longer. At least until nightfall. If he wasn't back by then, I'd know something bad had happened.

Sweat coated the uniform shirt and I stripped it off, looking around the room for something to do. The drawers to the dresser and end tables were empty and nothing else was present that stood out. I started with pushups, focusing on my training. Time passed. I went into sit-ups, squats, lunges—every exercise I could think of. I did set after set until so much time went by, I could barely move. Somehow, I found my way into the restroom and thanked God when water sputtered through the pipes. It evened out, pouring from the facet in a clear waterfall before I began cupping handfuls into my mouth and splashing my face. A loud bang had me jerking upright. I turned off the water as fast as I could.

"Fucking bullshit," a deep voice echoed in the distance. *"I'm gonna kill him. That fucking Master thinks he so much better than we are. I found him that slave. Me."*

"Quiet your ass down. I'm trying to pull patrol. You're going to scare the damn prisoners away."

"Fuck them. They can't get out of Whitlock. Besides, it's pointless. They're not even in this wing. Bet you anything they're held up in some Master's apartment holding him hostage or something."

"They're as good as dead if they touch a Master. Target practice," he said, laughing.

"Exactly. Now, back to what I was saying." I seethed at their coldness but kept myself grounded so my anger wouldn't win. The voices were practically outside as he continued. *"So, I wait for him to leave...he does. I knock on the door so Charlee can*

answer, and what happens? A guard. A fucking guard answers her door. But it's not one I've ever seen before. Some big, muscled motherfucker, as if that makes a difference."

"What did you say?"

"What do you think I said? I told him I needed to speak with Barclane. To have him contact me when he got home. And he did. He invited me over. I told him I was on leave from scouting and asked if I could offer my services, for free. He said, no, but thanks for the offer. And One, what does she do? Fucking raises her eyebrow at me all smug and shit. Bitch. When I get my hands on her, it's over. She's going to wish she never crossed me, and that's what she's doing—crossing me."

"Not a good situation, Fourteen. You know not to mix with Masters and slaves. It's forbidden."

A laugh filled the space and my brow creased. Fourteen? And he was a scout? Like Travis had been? *Fourteen ...*

I swallowed, and really looked at the tattoo on my chest for the first time. The numbers were small, but they could have been inches tall for the impact they suddenly left on me. 27011. Eleven. That was what they all called me. Everyone, but Nineteen. Yet he embraced his number with open arms. I couldn't understand it. In truth, I wasn't even really sure I understood him. I knew nothing about who he was. To hold a number as a name...it showed we were below titles. Unworthy of existence. Was I unworthy?

My eyes rose to the mirror, studying every aspect of my features—ones that had gotten me far in life. They made me popular. They brought attention from girls and women. They led to many opportunities like being the face of the MMA camp I had spent years training at. *They made me a slave.*

"Could be worse, I suppose. You could look like me."

Startled, I nearly launched myself in the direction of the voice. Nineteen seemed to notice and laughed as he dropped a large bag on the bed.

"Where the hell have you been? I thought you were captured. I was about to come looking for you."

"Damn guards." He pulled out a wrapped sandwich and a bag of chips, then tossed them at me. They're camping out at the entrance that leads here. I got lost trying to find my way around them. Pain in the ass, but at least I know two ways to get here now."

"How do you remember this shit? It's like you have a compass in your head. You keep finding all the right ways."

I tore open the wrapping and sunk my teeth into thick bread, turkey, ham, and veggies. My eyes nearly rolled in pleasure at the taste.

"Photographic memory. I only really have to see something once to recall details and shit. Check this out." He opened his own sandwich and smiled as he spouted out a long number.

"What's that?"

"The credit card number of the Master who was standing in line in front of me. Cool, right? I used it to pay for the food. Told the cashier I forgot my card and asked if she could type it in manually. She totally bought it."

"What?" I laughed, taking another bite. "Wait. They take credit cards here?"

Nineteen's face sobered. "Yeah. Scary, isn't it?"

"Scary? No, terrifying. It goes back to exactly what I suspected. The government has to know about this place. They have to. Fuck. Fuck." I was frozen in cascading questions. "How am I ever going to get Jessa out of here?"

"Who?"

"Jessa. She…she was my girlfriend. The three of us were taken. Me, my twin, and Jessa."

"But your twin is not here…right?"

"No." Speaking was nearly impossible. "We were at an island before we came here. She's there, and I plan to get her

124

back. But Jessa…she's here. If I leave without her…if I don't make it…"

"Don't think about that yet. You're getting way ahead of yourself. Right now, we focus on getting ourselves out of here. Once we do that, we can look for your sister."

"We?"

"That's right. You saved my life. I want to help in any way I can," he said, quieter.

"But what about you? Don't you want to go home? Isn't there—"

"There's no one," he said, cutting me off. "Dakota is dead. I'm Nineteen now, and I'm with you all the way. Two is better than one, wouldn't you say? We stick together."

I nodded, then headed with him to the bed. We sat on the edge, finishing our meal in silence. Even though my appetite was gone, I forced myself to eat. When Nineteen finished, he let out a sigh and turned to me.

"While I was stuck in the halls, I listened to the guards for a while. They're in groups and going in as teams to do a final sweep of floors one, two, and three. Tomorrow, they start with four through six. We're on the fourth floor. We'll have to find somewhere to go tonight. Either way, we're going to have to cross them. Sooner better than later, I say."

"I agree. The faster we can try to find a way out, the better."

"That might be a little hard. I overheard part of a conversation. It was with a man they call the high leader and someone I assume was a guard. I couldn't see them. Anyway, it didn't sound good. The high leader was angry, and yet worried. They were talking really quiet, but whatever is happening is causing the leader to leave no stone unturned. He even talked about tearing down walls. Something about secret passages. I'm half tempted to try to find one of those. Maybe it'll lead us out."

"Secret passages? You're kidding me."

"I'm not, but finding an entrance isn't going to be easy. I

don't even know where to begin. The dangerous part is, the high leader seemed to know. That's playing with fire."

I paused, turning to face him. "You could be right. If they're focusing on that aspect, we should probably avoid it."

"We're not safe anywhere. I don't like not having a plan. I feel like a rat in a maze. Nothing is for sure, and every turn could be our last."

"Did you hear anything else?"

"No. I wish I would have."

"Me too." I frowned, letting it all process. "Something is bugging me about the entire situation."

"What?" Growing quiet, Nineteen dug around in the bag, gazing up as he did.

"If they're searching floors one through three, why are guards still patrolling these halls? We're on the fourth floor, yet here they are. Why aren't they checking the rooms while they walk through? And our escape to begin with. None of it is right. Something is off."

"Dumb luck is my best guess on the escape. I'm not questioning that part. As for the guards, after what you did to the last one you encountered, maybe they're playing it safe and staying in large numbers."

"But they have guns."

A look crossed Nineteen's face that I couldn't read.

"Hell if I know. They sell us, right? Maybe they don't want to lose out on any money."

"Maybe."

"Anything happen while I was out?"

"Just two men talking. I think the guard called him Fourteen. He was a scout."

"Fourteen?" He was sitting straighter, more interested as he peered at me.

"That's right. Talking about a Master and how he got a guard to watch over his slave. Fourteen didn't sound too happy about that. Says the slave gave him a smug look and he was going to make her pay."

"Hmmm." A nod was all Nineteen gave as he pulled out a bag of candy. "Want one?"

"No thanks. I want to get out of here. I want to find a new place to stay."

Crinkling had me almost cringing as Nineteen shook his head. "It's way too risky to try to leave right now. If we're seen roaming the halls while a shitload of guards are doing searches, we're in big trouble."

"But you went down there. People saw you. And the guards aren't searching up here. They're doing exactly what you said, roaming the halls."

"I'm telling you, it's not that simple. Think about it. These men know each other. And even if they don't, there are men standing guard at the entrances at almost every turn. They're not walking around doing their own thing. They're working. They'll wonder why we're not working too."

Talking anymore was pointless. The more excuses I was given, the angrier I became. How could Nineteen sit back and eat candy with an expression that mirrored a man who was more confident than he should have been? We were slaves—prisoners. And we were on the run. For the first time since I'd bonded with him, I wasn't so sure putting my trust into this stranger was the best option. He appeared to care, but the truth was, everyone had their own agenda. What was his?

SCOUT 19

Questions. More questions. My only saving grace from more was the simple fact that I'd said we should rest, and Aamir actually obeyed. What was I going to do about all these sudden inquiries? And not just about our plan, or which way we'd be going, but about me. *My life. My family and upbringing.* I liked to think of myself as a semi-patient person, but with every question came more defensiveness. My role was slipping, and with it, my walls were lifting to keep him out. This was business. Aamir was not my friend, and he wasn't even really *Aamir*. He was Eleven. A slave. Perhaps it would have been better if I started forcing his identity on him. It's not like we were really getting free from Whitlock.

I pulled out the phone, checking the time. My heart jumped at the new message. And it wasn't from Mateo, but my Main Master. Quickly, I glanced over, easing from the closet as the light snores continued.

Sitting on the bed, I put my back to the cracked door and opened the alert.

MM: Things have changed. You bag one.

I blinked through shocked confusion. What was that

supposed to mean? Wasn't the purpose of this entire thing to protect the slave? To keep him alive until the auction? Now I didn't have to?

Nineteen: Bag one? A new slave?

A few minutes went by before a message was returned.

MM: Not a slave. You'll need to earn your money. Can't talk now. I'll message later.

My arms slowly lowered as I stared at the ground a few feet in front of me. Nothing was right about this mission. And I hated going into something I couldn't predict the outcome to. A bad feeling etched in, and no matter what I did to push it away, it wouldn't leave. *Bag one.* One person. So what of the slave? Was I still supposed to watch over him? Did I dump him back off at Slave Row and start a new mission?

"You found a phone?"

Eleven rushed around the bed as I clutched the cell tightly. It took sheer willpower to push my anger away and throw him a half-assed grin.

"It's impossible to unlock. I've been using it to tell the time. It's almost dead anyway."

"Why didn't you tell me this earlier?"

"Because I can't open it. It's useless."

A hard look overcame his face as he turned to the window.

"How much longer before we take off?"

I stuffed the phone in my pocket as I stood. I didn't care that light was still shining outside, or that the guards were most likely still searching the floors. This news had me anxious. I needed to move. *To do something.*

"Now. We've waited long enough. We'll just have to be careful."

"Let me slip on my boots."

Stuffing the trash from the store trip into the drawer of the bedside table, I scanned the room. I hadn't heard anyone outside for a while. I was pretty sure I could get us to the far reaches of the fortress without incident, but once we hit the decline, we were going to run into the real apartments. The ones filled with Masters and slaves. Anyone could see us. And I knew a few Masters. If they tried to have a conversation, I was screwed.

"Ready."

Apprehension mixed with anticipation as Eleven stared over at me. We were close to the same size, and I took him in for a few seconds. What would he do if my cover was exposed? Our situation could get bad fast. Especially since I couldn't kill him as a means to an end. I wasn't even sure I could if I wanted to. He was growing on me, and that wasn't good either.

"Stay close. If we run into anyone, stand tall. Be confident. You're a guard."

"Got it."

"Good. And if someone talks to us, go along with whatever I say. *No matter what it is.*"

"Okay."

The eagerness was there. I let out a pent-up breath, cracked open the door, and peeked my head through. The hall was clear, and I took off in a light jog as I headed in the direction opposite from the path I usually took. Eleven stayed only steps behind, mimicking my movements as we crouched while we ran.

The length of the hall was endless. We curved through the formation of the building and slowed as we approached the turn that would take us down to one of the main living quarters. As I hesitated, checking for guards, Eleven's hand came to rest on the center of my back. It had me looking over my shoulder and gesturing with my head that we were good to go.

A good one hundred yards went by before we approached the first door. I slowed to a fast, determined walk, and dropped back enough for Eleven to be at my side.

"Slow, but fast. We're not in a hurry, but we have a purpose. Does that make sense?"

"Yeah."

Screams came from the second door, and Eleven's head shot over. When we hit the fourth door, laughter poured free, as did pleas from a woman. There was more than one man. Two?

"Master!"

"I said down!"

"Jesus," Eleven breathed out. "This isn't—"

"Our concern," I said, glancing over and cutting him off. "Keep walking. Ignore it."

"Ignore it? You're kidding. You can't be that cold."

"Do you want out of here or not?"

He grew quiet, but I didn't have time to continue. Barclane and another Master were approaching, and he was staring right at me. My pulse jumped, but I didn't change my pace.

"Remember, follow my lead," I breathed out. "No matter what."

Eleven didn't respond before Barclane's hand rose and his finger came to point at me. Seconds went by as we got within feet of each other.

"You have some explaining to do."

"Not right now I don't, Master. We're on business." My eyes cut and hinted to the supposed guard at my side. Barclane glanced in Eleven's direction, his brow creasing as he seemed to catch that something was off.

"Perhaps not. Business, you say? What better business than providing your services to the people who employ you?" He gestured his head to a tall, older man wearing a suit at his side. There was a refined elegance to his appearance, but I saw past it. "Join us. The high leader tells me there are slaves missing. Being a member of the Whitlock board, I demand to know what's going on."

"I would rather the high leader fill you in. I'm not qualified to—"

"Just a few questions."

Tightly, my jaw clenched. "As you wish."

He gestured to the door he was standing by, and the man pulled out a key, unlocking and opening it. Eleven's chest rose and fell at a fast pace as he stole glances at me. He was on the verge of attacking. I could see the bloodlust in his eyes. He wanted nothing more than to kill these men. It was the same look I'd seen before with many of the guards and scouts at Whitlock.

"Calm. Don't do anything rash. This won't take long."

My words were barely audible, but he nodded and took his position behind me as we entered the apartment. A white leather sofa rested over hardwood floors and glass tables decorated the space and dining room. The only thing that stood out was a tiny pink velvet chair. What sat in it had Eleven's hand locking on my forearm with a strength that had me nearly groaning in pain. A girl with nearly-white long hair sat straight and poised. Pink bows rested on each side of her head, and her bangs stopped just short of her big, round eyes. Pale ivory covered her porcelain face and a heart was colored amid the center of her lips in soft pink. Where her cheekbones angled rested two pink circles, the same shade as the lipstick. White lace fluffed around her biceps and was tightly fitted over her flat chest. The length barely came to cover pale thighs. Black shoes shined from the reflective light and just above them was a pair of white socks with the same sort of frilly lace she was adorned in.

Movement was non-existent. She barely blinked while she stared ahead as still as the doll she was supposed to be. I doubted she spoke or walked anywhere. Her legs were thin, devoid of any muscle tone. Could she stand if she wanted to? Did he feed her to keep her alive, or did she feed herself? My questions were mirrored by Eleven's horror-filled stare. But it wasn't on the girl anymore. There were two more, just as still, sitting on the floor behind the sofa, leaning against the counter separating the kitchen. One was a brunette, while the other had dark ebony skin. Both had big eyes, frozen in terror. Their pale yellow and blue lace dresses were torn in locations, and old, dry blood stained the fragile fabric. Their skin, down to the gaping wound on one's neck and the other's breast, appeared to be wax. They were dead, and my guess, given the dullness of their clothing, it had been for quite some time.

"Two prisoners, slaves now, thanks to the Main Master," Barclane said, drawing my attention as I shook Eleven's grip loose, "are on the run. Hiding somewhere within these walls. It's inexcusable. Absurd they got loose from the White Room to begin with. You got a description of them?"

"Two males."

When I didn't continue, Barclane's eyes narrowed. He glanced at Eleven suspiciously. "Two males. And? Maybe *elaborate*."

"I can't do that. We weren't there or part of the search. We're supposed to be on our way to Guard Quarters. We really can't be late. Perhaps if you called on the high leader again, he can better explain."

"No. I want to hear what you know. Besides, he won't mind. Not if you're with me." Barclane glanced at the other man who was now petting the crown of the girl's head. "Tell me, Master King. You overlook the guard and scouting at Whitlock. Do the number of guards we have cover shifts if one or two happen to be late?"

"Easily. Give me a minute and I'll call so they're aware of the situation."

"Excellent."

The man pulled out his phone while Barclane grabbed my bicep, pulling me to the far side of the room. Eleven's face was tight with anger and concern. He was seconds away from reacting, but seemed to calm as I put my hand out to the side so he'd know it was okay.

"What the fuck are you still doing here? You didn't answer my calls. You're supposed to be out of the country."

"I'm undercover," I ground out, quietly. "It's deeper than

scouting. I believe the Main Master has found his slave via information from another Master residing here. The only way I'll know for sure is if I blend in amongst the guard. *Main Master Whitlock doesn't even know I'm still here.*"

"Be blunt. I'm not playing some guessing game with you. Who is this Master, and where did he say she was? And why the hell would posing as the guard help you pull this off?"

I let his own conversation with the CIA director come back. "I don't know who he is, only what I overheard. He said she may be off the island of Crete and he's going to go there. He's asking for two guards to accompany him on his journey to find out. I mean for us to be those two guards. Can we go now?"

"Crete, you say?" He grew quiet, letting his stare drop to the ground before bringing it back up to Eleven. For a long moment, he studied him, narrowing his eyes as he did. I quickly cut in, trying to distract him.

"I should be able to call after we leave tomorrow night. I'll keep in touch."

"Wait. Who is that? He's young. Too young, and too...*good looking.*"

"He's just a guard. No one special."

"You lie. You're both unarmed. You're not even wearing duty belts. You're the slaves they're looking for, aren't you? *He* is a slave. What were those numbers the high leader mentioned? *Numbers.*"

Barclane paused at his nearly silent words, going rigid as his eyes widened. Faster, my heart raced.

"You." His hand rose, pointing to Eleven. "I know you."

Shifting, Eleven shook his head. "Not sure what you mean. I'm new here. I don't think we've met."

I was left as Master Barclane headed forward. "We haven't officially met, no, but I know all about you and your sister. Your twin. I'm Master Barclane. Have you heard of me?"

Rapid blinking was followed by Eleven's lips separating. My

head shook, but Master King's hand clamped on my shoulder just as fast. The strength behind the hold had self-preservation soaring. I knew the dangers we were in.

"*Barclane?*"

"That's right. Think real hard. Has anyone ever mentioned my name to you?"

Eleven's breaths grew heavy as a battle played over his face. "You were going to help Mistress Harper. You…were going to get an apartment for me and Layla. You're the Mistress's friend."

"No!" I broke free, lunging toward them. There was a gun in my face so fast, instinct had me jerking to a stop, inches away from the man I had ratted out to the Main Master.

"Is this part of your scheme? We're working together, and I expect the entire truth. Is this how you plan to lure her out? With her slave as bait?"

I found myself remaining silent as I nodded through the betrayal on Eleven's face.

"Nineteen …you're working with this Master? But…I thought you were a…you said—"

"Enough," I snapped. "*What did I tell you?*"

The gun lowered, and Barclane laughed as he threw King a quick glance. "She'll take the bait. Great work, Nineteen. What do you need? You need out of here? I can get you a car ready and have you flown to Crete right now."

"Did you miss the part where I'm going with another Master? This is bigger than I can explain. It's imperative we accompany him."

Suspicion had his jaw tightening. "Is that so? Because I would think if you were working for me, this other Master would be irrelevant. Especially if I could get you to her. Perhaps we're still unclear on some things." He paused, his lips twisting as he reached into his pocket to withdraw a small ring of keys. "I'm getting hungry. How about you and I go back to my place and grab a quick bite to eat? We can talk while we do.

I'm sure Master King wouldn't mind keeping an eye on our dear slave."

"We shouldn't be talking in the first place. Especially in the apartments."

"Don't be absurd. There's nothing wrong with us sharing conversation over a quick little snack. Besides, I've gotten tired of being watched. I've taken care of it."

"I have nothing else to tell you."

"Nineteen?"

There was a threat coming from Eleven—one I knew was going to be deadly to someone if I didn't think of something fast.

"Just a quick bite. *I insist.*"

BRAM

Sleep beckoned but wouldn't come. I was too avaricious to miss a moment of Everleigh's presence, yet too exhausted to stay awake completely. Light traces of nails made a path over my chest and every inch of me tingled as traces of the drug made itself known in the deep recesses within. I went through periods of being back to normal, and moments where I felt like I weighed a million pounds. It took everything I had to turn and bury my face in my slave's neck as she continued to caress my bicep.

"Do you have to leave? Can't you just stay and take care of everything from here?"

The laugh was soft as her hand paused at the top of my shoulder.

"It's not time."

"Tell me what you want me to do."

Silence lasted for so long, sleep began to win over. A hum vibrated my body, and my heartbeat exploded in surprise as her whispered tone jolted me awake.

"I'm afraid we're in trouble. Something isn't right."

Light broke through as I forced my eyes open. "What do you mean?"

"I don't know. I've spent my days going over everything. And not just from when I left. Before then. Before West. Over the course of his reign and death, to you taking back over, I've tried to keep track of these Masters as best as I could without being here. And it helps seeing who they represent on the outside world, but..." She swallowed hard, lifting to a sitting position. The concern had me following her actions, regardless that I was more tired than ever.

"Outside world. You have to tell me what you know. I can't do anything if I don't know. I'm blind out there. Dead to that world."

Blue eyes met mine, and she frowned, turning more to face me.

"You can't help me, Bram. The best thing you can do is help yourself. *Here*, at Whitlock. You can't trust any of them. Not a single person."

"I don't. You have to know that."

Her lips parted as she paused. "The amount you distrust them, double it. Trust them less than that." She shifted uneasily. "I have men in your guard."

"Men? My men?"

"*Our men*. They are not disloyal to you, but loyal to me as well as you. Do you understand? They hear things. They protect you more than you know."

My head shook as her words refused to make sense in my mind. "No one has said anything to me. If they know something, shouldn't they be telling *me*?"

"No," she said, softly. "You've been too unstable. It wasn't safe. They tell me."

"And what do they tell you?"

Everleigh stood from the bed and headed for the dresser. All her clothes were still there. I never doubted she'd be back. As she pulled out new undergarments, she slowly faced me. The worry was real. So much so, my need to protect her drew me from the bed.

"Before I say anything, let me ask you a question. Who at Whitlock do you trust the most?"

"Easy. Derek, my high leader. He was with me throughout my recovery. He's as loyal as I'm going to find."

The nod was slow. Without a word, she turned and headed to the adjoining bathroom. I followed, not understanding what she was getting at. When the shower started, only then did she meet my gaze.

"Slave, speak. I don't have the patience for riddles. Especially after being drugged. I can't think."

Everleigh placed the undergarments on the counter and lifted herself to sit next to the sink as she beckoned me forward with her finger. The first kiss to my lips was light, increasing as her one good arm wrapped around my neck, pulling me in closer.

"I've always protected you when I could, haven't I?"

"Yes."

"So, if I told you you have to replace your high leader, would you?"

"I need him. Everleigh, be blunt. Tell me what you've heard."

"I saw his reaction, Bram. I saw you threaten him and his response. He doesn't like this. Like *me*, or us together. I have a feeling I can't shake about him. We watch these Masters. We try to beat them at this game, but perhaps we're worrying about the wrong people." Her lips tightened through some emotion I couldn't place. It was a mix of anger, yet something darker. "There's so much to all those involved. What I do know is you must distance him from leadership. Replace him immediately."

"I told you, I need him. I can't do that."

"Then I fear for you. *I fear for us.*"

Everleigh eased me back and lowered from the counter to

head to the shower. I followed, hating how her fears brought out the beast in me. It left me on the cusp of murderous irrationality. I'd kill to extinguish her worries. To never let her feel another ounce of uncertainty again. And I would do it without question. The person or place didn't matter.

"Stay. Stay and I'll change my plan. We can come up with one together."

Warm water splashed against me, and I shut the glass door as Everleigh stepped into the stream, protecting the bandage on her shoulder. She watched my every move, just as I watched hers. My legs were shaky, but my eyes were clear. Each expression she made, every scan from my eyes to my lips, brought back the desperate obsession. I didn't have to tell her a word as she met me halfway, crushing her lips to mine.

"I can't. Replace him before it's too late."

"*Stay.*"

Our words were said between our hunger. Spinning her to the wall, I grabbed my cock, needing to be back inside her. Nothing felt more important than that and the realization had me slowing. She'd be gone soon. I had to get control of this. What we were talking about couldn't be delayed.

"I'll be a dead man if I let him go. You don't understand. You have things you're not telling me, and I have my way of dealing with what's happening here. If you were at my side, you'd see that. Watching over a camera isn't the same. I need you, Everleigh. Letting Derek go will have everything falling apart. I stand no chance if he—"

"We have options. For one, there's a guard. He's loyal to both of us. *He* can keep you safe."

"A guard? You mean you've already picked out a new high leader? Without consulting me? We could have done that together. *Together*, slave."

For the first time since her return, anger exploded within me. I froze, glaring down as I tried to process her motives. Was it to truly keep us both safe, or was there more? I trusted Everleigh to an extent. I didn't believe she'd try to kill me so she could have Whitlock, but I didn't like her taking control over what was rightfully mine either.

"Why are you looking at me like that?"

Putting distance between us, all I could do was show my bewilderment to her question. "Why? Do you hear what you're saying?"

"Yes. We're both in danger, and I'm trying to keep us safe."

"And you didn't think to maybe talk to me about everything first? You don't think I can keep us safe?"

The lack of response said it all. A shocked laugh left me as the heat intensified within.

"I'm not saying you can't keep us safe. I'm saying while you've been looking for me, I've spent every day—countless hours—digging into the people who are here. Whether they're intentions toward us are good or not, I needed to know. Hell, I may know more about them than you do."

"You think so? Then tell me, slave. What have you learned that you think puts us at so much risk? What do you know that I don't?"

Everleigh grabbed the soap and lathered her body as if I hadn't just asked her the five-hundred-million-dollar question.

"Well? I'm waiting."

"I need to rinse."

"No, you need a good spanking. You have ten seconds to start talking."

I moved out of the way, letting her maneuver herself in the water. My arms were crossed over my chest and my brain was finally getting through the haze of the drug. A yawn left me, and I couldn't stand it.

"You've allowed two women into Whitlock as Mistresses."

My jaw tightened as I stood taller. "I have. Their connections were impressive. They're in need of an outlet. I have their outlet

141

here. Besides, one of the Mistresses I happened to go to college with. I trust her. Enough so, all I had to do was mention your slave and she didn't hesitate to help break him out."

"What do you know of them?"

"What does this have to do with Derek or...anyone?"

Everleigh lathered her hair, giving me a look. "We're all connected in one way or another. Did you know one was the former mistress to your second-in-charge, the CIA Director? He had an affair with Katia Marchase just after he got his position. Did you also know she's blackmailing him? He would have had her killed, of course, if she weren't so powerful. If you ask me, my money is on her. She may just kill him first, here, at Whitlock."

"You mean, my money?"

Her smile fell as she pursed her lips.

"Are you not listening?"

"Of course I am. And fine, okay, no, I wasn't aware they had an affair. I did know they were acquaintances. Continue."

"Thank you." She stepped aside, switching places with me as she took a deep breath. "As I was saying, this Katia woman is very well protected. I could barely get anything on her. She and the other woman, Elaine, are connected, but I'm not quite sure how. Same college, but my sources say they weren't necessarily friends. It's very odd. Even odder, they both call themselves Jane. Why would they say their name is Jane to strangers?"

"No idea. Should I be worried about them?"

"No. I don't think so. It's the men you have to worry about. Your entire board has their own motives. Luckily, one of them is mine."

"Yours? As in he's an informant for you?"

"Precisely. He keeps me in the loop."

"*And which member is this?*"

There was hesitancy as she handed me the body soap.

"Slave?"

"Master King. He tells me Barclane has a scout after me. Many are plotting to have me killed before I can return. Barclane thinks I donated money to have him exposed."

It was my turn to pause. "Word travels fast."

"So, you knew?"

"I donated the money. I had to know where he stood concerning you. As for the scout, he's one of mine. He's the one who told me."

"What will you do to Barclane?"

I finished rinsing and shut off the shower as I opened the door and got us towels. Everleigh didn't take her stare from me as she dried herself off and put on her lace panties and bra. Going through our routine, it was a quiet staring match. I watched her in the mirror as I brushed my teeth, and she watched me as she did the same. When we were finished, I gestured to the room.

"Barclane...I need him right now. When that changes, he's yours. Now, tell me more about Derek and the others."

"There's nothing other to say than he's bad news. So is Mateo. He is dirty, and he's with the ones who do not have you or Whitlock's best interest in mind."

"I'm very aware of Mateo breaking the rules and making scouting deals behind my back."

"And you're okay with that?"

"Absolutely not."

Everleigh was hot on my trail as I came to a stop at the dresser. Her impatience for me to elaborate nearly had me smiling as I put on my briefs and headed to the closet. I didn't say a word as I took out a suit and began putting it on.

"What then? What will you do?"

"About what?"

She threw me an aghast look. "About Mateo. About Derek and your board members? King is fine, for now. The rest are not.

You have to clean house. There's no other way around it. We're both as good as dead if you don't."

"What do you propose I do, Everleigh? Kill them all and be done with it? I did that with the last board. Did it teach these new members not to cross me? No. It only made them try harder to hide things. There are other ways."

"Like what?"

I slid on my shoes and forced a grin as I took her hands in mine and drew her close. "We'll talk about it tonight. Right now, there's someone I want you to meet. Formally. *With me.*"

"Alvin."

Everleigh was already smiling as I nodded. "He's probably wondering where I am. I'm a little surprised I haven't heard him banging around out there. Get dressed. We'll be waiting for you."

AAMIR

I had made a lot of mistakes in my life, but somewhere within me, I knew this wasn't going to be one of them. With Master Barclane only feet away, and Nineteen on his other side, Master or not, I knew I couldn't let him separate us. Even if Nineteen was one of them, something told me I was better off with him than without. I couldn't let my anger over his lies overshadow that. *I needed him.*

"It'll only be a few minutes. Master King will take good care of the slave."

My eyes darted to the doll-girl sitting like a statue in the chair. To know she had been a regular girl, someone's daughter, and what she had become, I took a step closer to the door. Barclane glanced at me, and I shook my head. Not just to try to erase the horrors of what I had seen at this point, but to him.

"I'm not staying in this place. Nineteen and I are together. We're leaving here together. *Nineteen…*"

He immediately took a step closer to me, only for Barclane's arm to bar over his chest like a gate. Nineteen's actions were so fast, I barely had time to take in his hand locking on the Master's wrist. With a hard squeeze, the gun fell from the older man's grip and Nineteen had it before it dropped a few inches.

"We're leaving. I told you what I could. Take it or leave it. Know what you want will be accomplished. How I get that done is up to me."

I grabbed the knob and threw open the door as Nineteen stormed past, pulling me with him. I didn't bother to shut the barrier behind me. We were both moving at a swift pace and looking over our shoulders as Barclane lunged through the doorway, stopping in the hall to glare at us. The moment we rounded the turn, Nineteen pulled at my shirt so I could take off at a fast run with him. Random doors opened, but we didn't slow until we were entering another passage.

"Fuck. Fuck," he growled, holstering the gun. "We have to find cover."

"Wrong. *I'm leaving.* We part ways once I figure how to escape this place."

Angry eyes cut over. "Don't be stupid. You're screwed without me."

I grabbed Nineteen's shoulders and slammed him into the wall as my fury grew. "You're on their side! You're using me. What for? To catch the Mistress like you told Barclane?"

My arm went numb, exploding in pain as Nineteen brought his elbow down on my lower bicep and stepped free.

"I have no idea what the fuck I'm doing. All I know is I'm to protect you. That's the truth. In the meantime—"

Screams cut him off. Both our heads shot over as a door floor open and a blur hit and bounced off the white wall a few feet down. Red stained the stone surface, matching the drenched heap resting on the floor. Just as fast as the barrier opened, it closed, leaving me staring in a stunned silence.

"We have to go. The guards will come collect her soon."

"Her?"

Somehow, I knew it was a person, but I couldn't process

what I was seeing. The small red ball in a fetal position didn't look like a woman or girl. It looked like a...*child.*

"*Let's go.*"

The tug had me jerking back. I took a few steps, only to come to a stop as a broken-up breath had the girl's shoulders lifting with the gurgling intake. Dark hair splayed over her face and an array of different shades of red masked the surface. I lowered, ignoring Nineteen's curse.

"*Eleven*, we have to go. She's dead."

"Don't call me that. She's not. She's trying to breathe."

"That's not a breath. Not like you think."

Seconds went by before the gurgling shook her body once again.

"She's dead. Haven't you ever seen a dead body before? This is what it does when you die. Look."

Nineteen crouched, grasping the girl's shoulder and pushing her to her back. Limp limbs fell to her sides and blank eyes met mine as her head rolled. She took what appeared to be another breath. Teeth indents led to a chunk missing from her swollen cheek and a crater was evident on the far side of her forehead. The location was so close to where Layla had been injured, I immediately gagged. The girl couldn't have been of legal age. She was tiny, and young.

"Dead. Now, let's go."

"Go? You're not going anywhere without taking that bitch with you."

I never heard the door open. My brain couldn't even take in the man's appearance. All I knew was I was up and lunging right for him. Sound disappeared, and like the pop of a rubber band, stark features flooded in: bulging brown eyes, a large, wide nose, and thin lips parted in surprise. Crashing from the lamp echoed in the distance and more cursing came as I slammed my fist into the man's face. He stumbled back, keeping on his feet as he tried to steady himself from falling over the side of the sofa.

An arm wrapped around my waist, pulling me back, but I put every ounce of my strength into planting myself so I could swing again. My impact was crushing, quickly followed by another blow. Somehow, I was lifted and spun in the opposite direction. Nineteen's arms tightened around me while I went crazy trying to break his hold and get to the unconscious man on the floor.

"Enough. *Enough!*"

Action was all I knew. Revenge. These men didn't deserve to live.

"Get a grip, man. *Eleven.* Think of Layla. Do you want out of here or not?"

Layla…*yes.* Layla could be in danger like this. She could be hurt or even on the verge of death. The thought did nothing to calm me. It left me worse, and hungry for increased violence.

"Get off me!"

A hard squeeze followed, but Nineteen let go. The door was shut, and a putrid smell had me blinking through the cloud of rage. I spun, scanning the dirty apartment while I tried to think. Blood was smeared over the tan sofa and dark splotches tinted the carpet. From the look, some appeared old, while others were clearly new. Blood stains. Blood. *The girl.* Layla.

"We have to leave. Someone is going to see that girl if he hasn't already called the guard to come get her. We're running out of time."

Moaning had me looking toward the Master on the floor. Panic at Nineteen's words registered, but I couldn't erase those dead eyes I had stared into…those hallow, yet restricted breaths. These men…they weren't just sick. What they were doing went far beyond that. Whitlock was the elite landfill for the diabolical garbage dump.

"Mmmm."

A groan filled the space and I reared back, sending the steel toe of the boot smashing into his mouth and nose. Once. Twice. A growl poured from Nineteen, but he didn't stop me. I kicked at the man's face like my life depended on it. And in some twisted way, it had. If I got caught, I'd return to Slave Row. Some Master or Mistress would kill me for their own enjoyment.

"Fuck, this isn't happening. None of this is right."

Nineteen's fingers fisted in his hair, and he spun as I stomped on the man's throat with all my might.

"No, it's not. None of it. You..." I growled. "You should be dead like him. *You knew.* You let this continue and did nothing. Even now, you do nothing!"

"Do you know where you are? Do you know who runs this place, or who occupies it, for that matter? *No.* Whatever you think you may accomplish by getting out, you better think again. Whitlock...there's no bringing it down. The very people you'd run to are the same ones who are looking to own you. *To kill you.* If you ever did manage to escape, your best bet would be to disappear. Never breathe a word of what you know or what you've seen. A mere mention is a manifestation of your worst nightmare. They hear. They see. Even now, *they watch.*" Nineteen stepped closer, pointing to the dead Master on the floor. "What you just did is the death sentence you escaped. You fool! You were cleared, and now you've put yourself back in the White Room. Do you know who you just killed?"

"If you think I care about this piece of shit—"

"A major archbishop, Eleven. One of four *in the world.* Do you think just anyone can come here? Each door you cross is accompanied by our country's rulers, corporate gods, and celebrities. Anyone who is in a position to matter is here. *Do you see?* Can you even grasp what I'm telling you?"

"The media? What if I went public and exposed everything?"

A small laugh followed the shaking of his head. "You really are clueless. I'm assuming you're referring to major media outlets, in which I'd tell you, they're bought and paid for by our government to control what the public knows. You'd be dead the moment Whitlock left your lips."

Tears burned my eyes and I forced myself to swallow back the helplessness that took over.

"What about other countries?"

"Are you seriously asking me that? Where were you before here? We're networked. These places are everywhere."

"No."

"*Yes*. There is no winning. The best chance you have for change is to change it here. Bram Whitlock knows that. Everleigh Harper knows as well. Why do you think they fear her return?"

Before I could think to answer, heavy boots sounded from the outside.

"Not a word," Nineteen rushed out.

"They'll just pick up the body, right?"

"Shhh." Nineteen slowly locked the door, moving closer to me. "They should. We'll be fine. Remember, if anything happens, let *me* handle it."

I threw him a glare but stayed quiet as light talking began. My heart raced, and I closed my eyes, trying to ignore the stench that kept turning my stomach. For a man of purity, of supposed cleanliness of the body and soul, he was dirty in not only his actions, but his lifestyle.

"*You grab her. I picked up the last one.*"

"*Fuck that. I've been here longer than you. It's part of the job.*"

"*This part sucks. I want to be on the search.*"

"*Grab the damn slave.*"

Knock. Knock.

"Go away!"

Nineteen's voice was deep as he yelled out.

Silence was met with his order and the seconds dragged out torturously before he eased to the door and looked out the peephole. When he waved me over, I went forward with emotions I couldn't process. So many things were going through my mind.

So many hopes died with each step to his side. Layla and I would never be free. Even if I did manage to pull off a miracle and get her off Red Island, we'd be like the Mistress they searched for—always on the run. Never free. Forever hunted by the people meant to keep us safe.

SCOUT 19

From the moment I walked into my Main Master's office to confess Master Barclane's proposition, I was doomed. This mission was doomed. Everything was shit. This part was supposed to be the easiest. One task: protect the slave. Right. I had all but failed, and not by letting people get to him, but protecting him from himself.

"Slow down."

My command came out harsh, but Eleven obeyed. He was wired. Balancing on the deep end of some episode I didn't even want to consider. Maybe I shouldn't have told him the truth about how this place worked, but I figured, deep down, he already knew. Besides, I doubted he would ever leave these walls. The Main Master wasn't stupid. He may have been letting Eleven run around now, but if he wanted us captured for real, we wouldn't stand a chance.

"Where are we going?"

I glanced over, unsure how to answer. Slowing at the next intersecting hall, I stayed quiet as I peered down the length.

"Nineteen?"

"Just…wait."

"You have to have some idea. We can't just stay in these halls."

"There's a place, but…I don't think we'll be safe there. I'm not sure we really are anywhere."

My teeth clenched, and I pulled out the phone. The background lit up at my push and I cursed. Bram told me he'd contact me later. His message was cryptic as fuck and left me more confused than ever.

"Are you working for him? For the Main Master?"

At my silence, he only got angrier.

"Don't play stupid with me. He told me I was going to help him, and I wouldn't even know it. Are you working for the Main Master? It's a simple question." A moment passed before Eleven shoved into my shoulder. "That's what I fucking thought. What is his goal for allowing this right now? Is it supposed to help him with the Mistress? Is my running around meant to draw her in? Just…*tell me*. Tell me what you know."

"That's the thing, I know nothing other than to keep you safe."

"Why don't you fucking ask him then? You've got a phone. Call him."

"Are you crazy? I can't just *call* him. He's the Main Master. He gave me orders. I plan to follow them."

Eleven's hands came to his hips as he eyed the phone and glanced over to my gun. Training had me taking a step back.

"You try going for either one and I'll break your hand. Don't be any stupider than you already have been. If you try to hurt me or go off on your own, we both know you won't make it far. You don't know where you're going."

"Then lead. Preferably to the fucking exit of this shithole."

"It's not that simple."

I began to walk again while Eleven followed. For the life of me, I couldn't return the phone to my pocket. I needed to speak with the Main Master. I needed to tell him about the major archbishop Eleven had killed, and how Barclane exposed who I was.

The elevation began to drop, and I veered us left toward my grandfather's apartment—the one that should have been mine. We weren't too far from Slave Row or Medical, more on the opposite side of the White Room. Just as we made it to the entrance of more apartments, voices had me jolting to a stop. My arm shot out and I pushed Eleven to the opposite side of the entrance.

"Pull guard. Stare ahead and don't say a word. Don't look at them," I said, almost inaudible.

Eleven mirrored me, stiffening his posture as a Master, two guards, and a woman holding a child's hand came around the turn. The boy caught my attention and I recognized them instantly from being in the Main Master's quarters.

"Two guards? Here? What is this?"

The Master slowed, and the guards eyed me questionably.

"Code orange, sir. The slaves have yet to be recovered. The high leader fears they may be in the immediate area."

"Orange? Odd. I didn't authorize that."

The man's voice clicked, and my adrenaline spiked as I recognized it from the abandoned lobby. The Master—the CIA director. He was the one who had Everleigh Harper's location in Crete. He wanted her dead.

"I'm just following orders from the high leader. I think something may have happened."

"But he just left me, and he didn't think to mention anything. Unless..." Anger flashed, and he let out a sound as he threw the guards a look.

"Perhaps we should get the woman and boy back, Master Hunt." The dark-haired guard didn't take his eyes off me as he spoke. "The Main Master will be upset if he finds out the high leader left their side. They're not to be parted."

"But parted under the circumstance for good reason. Did you

not just hear the guard? Something's happened, just like I told the high leader it would. Be glad he went to check headquarters like I suggested. These prisoners are obviously very dangerous. The boy is safe with me. Once I grab some stuff from my apartment, we'll take him back."

"We were only supposed to go to Medical. Alvin shouldn't be roaming the halls like this."

"Are you speaking, *slave?*" Master Hunt threw the woman a glare, silencing her. I could see all their discomfort and knew the guards weren't comfortable putting their foot down. Something was wrong. Very, very wrong.

"Actually…" I glanced at Eleven. "Didn't you say the high leader mentioned a transport?"

Eleven's lips parted as he took in the group. "Yes. He did mention that."

"Now it makes sense." I shrugged, shaking my head to Master Hunt. "New guy. I swear to God, he's going to get me in fucking trouble. The high leader must have meant for us to transport the boy and woman back. You can go get your things. We can take it from here."

"Absolutely not. The boy is fine. We'll get him back."

"I'm sure you could, but an order is an order, Master Hunt."

"Do you know who I am?"

I nodded as the guards shifted behind him. "I do, actually, and I'm sorry, but I follow my high leader and Main Master, and this boy is his, not yours. Shall we go?"

"You can't talk to me like that."

I ignored Master Hunt as the guard eyeing me nodded in approval and pushed his hand to the middle of the older slave woman's back. We headed in the opposite direction while I prayed Eleven kept his cool. Two doors went by before the guard's suspicion grew and he moved back between me and Eleven.

"Take my place."

He didn't wait for Eleven to obey. He grabbed his arm, shoving him in the front. My fingers twitched to grab my gun, but composure came as he moved in closer.

"I know you. You're Nineteen. You're a scout, and he's no guard. What the hell is going on? False patrols, whispers between the Masters? What are they not telling us?"

"I don't know," I said, honestly. "My position is confidential. But I do need to see the Main Master, and I need you both to get me there without shit getting crazy. What happened with the high leader?"

The guard let out an exasperated sound. "Fuck if I know. One minute we're leaving Medical. Then he and the *snake* start whispering. The next thing we know, the high leader is taking off saying it's urgent."

"You called Master Hunt a snake."

"Damn right I did. If you ask me, he purposely ran our high leader off. Can you think of another reason he'd want to get a little boy alone in his apartment? You know they don't run this young here anymore. I think he caused that diversion."

Eleven glanced back at us, but thankfully stayed quiet as we headed down a new hall.

"The boy will be safe now, and I'll let the Main Master know to keep his eye on Master Hunt."

"Be sure to do that. I don't know what the hell is going on with all of this, but if this were real, we would have had y'all within an hour of your escape. Mateo, the scout leader, advised us to stick to the halls versus the room. He said this behind the high leader's back. That in itself threw a red flag to most of us."

"It's complicated. The entire thing is."

"Well, when you figure it out, you owe me an explanation. The last few months have been a fucking roller coaster. People who run this place are dying every damn day. Masters, guards. It's out of control. All because of her—a slave."

"Slave?" The guard who had remained quiet turned to throw

the other behind him a look. "Did you ever meet that slave? Did you see what she went through with Master Harper? I did. That *slave* turned Mistress has more backbone than anyone I've ever met. The price she paid married to Master Harper was one you couldn't imagine. So, the Main Master loves her. I don't blame him. I can see why he would."

"Are you on her side too?"

The disbelief rang out in the guard's tone next to me, but with no answer, he just shook his head.

"See. Everything is going to shit. Everything. This is not the Whitlock way. This is not what I signed up for."

Guards appeared in the distance, and I pulled Eleven's sleeve to bring him closer to me. The man at my side took his place in the front and it was almost impossible to remain calm. It was the first checkpoint before we entered the numerous halls leading to the Main Master's quarters. Every intersection after that was sure to have posted guards waiting to find something not quite right. We were sitting ducks, headed to the one place we shouldn't have been going.

BRAM

The bedrooms, the living room, the kitchen…Alvin and Ms. Pat were nowhere to be found. I spun in a circle, heading to the stairs and taking two at a time as I called out their name. Everleigh's voice echoed behind me, but disappeared just as fast as I burst into the hallway and started throwing open the doors. I knew she had headed back down, but I couldn't think about anything but the safety of the little boy I was now responsible for. Fear twisted in my gut, and I pushed myself faster as I headed back to the main floor.

"No. *The boy*. I want him found, and I want him found now." Everleigh paused from talking on her phone as I rushed into my office and threw on the light. For having one of the fastest computers, my fingers weren't working nearly as quick as they usually did. A child. A child who was mine in every right here at Whitlock, and he could be amongst the monsters. One could be hurting him this very second.

"Yes. Alvin. He's with the older slave woman, and maybe, more than likely, the high leader. That's right."

Cameras popped up on my screen and I browsed the last ones

I had up: Master Barclane, Master Hunt, and Master King. No Alvin.

"What do you mean he's there with you?" Everleigh asked, shocked.

"Who?" My head shot up. "Who's where?"

Everleigh shifted nervously on her feet. "The high leader is in the barracks. He's talking to some of the guards. Yelling at them. Alvin isn't with him."

"No," I growled. "Fuck. Fuck! He's not supposed to leave his side."

Blue disappeared as Everleigh closed her eyes, resting her palm against her forehead. "No. Walk it back." She paused, looking at me. "You too, Bram, walk it back. Rewind the tape and find when he left. Trace his steps and do it fast."

She was talking, but I was already in the process of typing in the time I went into my room. Black and white appeared and blurred through the high speed as I hit fast-forward. My throat nearly closed as I saw Ms. Pat lead him into the kitchen. The meal lasted seconds before she got him ready and they left with Derek and two guards.

"Wait. You're sure?"

Medical appeared as I tracked their steps. Alvin was getting seen by his doctor. Ease began to take over as Everleigh hung up the phone.

"They're almost here. Alvin is okay. I'm afraid there's a situation concerning the guards escorting him, though."

I hit the button, stopping just as they began leaving the medical room. My breaths were heavy, and my hands were shaking. Concern masked Everleigh's face. I didn't need to know her thoughts to read them. Alvin wasn't safe at Whitlock. Not without added precautions. Derek. I had trusted him to stay with Alvin and he hadn't. That was something I was going to have to deal with immediately.

"I could take him," Everleigh said, softly. "*We could take him...leave here forever.*"

"You know I can't allow either of those."

Full lips pressed together, and her eyes dropped to my chest. Before we could speak again, the front door opened. I didn't wait to rush out so I could see Alvin for myself. What I wasn't expecting was for two guards to accompany Ms. Pat inside. I barely gave them notice as I met her with a hard stare.

"You didn't inform me Alvin needed to go to Medical. Is he sick?"

Her mouth parted in fear as Alvin broke away and ran to my waiting arms.

"He has a slight cough and congestion. I didn't think it was anything to worry you over. I...I..." She sniffled, looking down.

"You what?"

"Main Master, if we may..."

Irritation almost had me snapping, until I realized I was looking at familiar faces.

"Well, isn't this a surprise."

Nineteen came forward, but my attention wasn't on him. It was on Eleven's shocked face as Everleigh left my office and walked past me.

"*You're here.*" A ragged breath left him, only for the slave to shake his head. "I can't believe you're here. He found you? You're at Whitlock for good?"

"I'm afraid not. I'm actually glad you're here. We need to talk, Eleven."

"Ever-leigh!"

Alvin wiggled, and I let him go to her as I tried to get a grip on the sudden emotions colliding with my anger. Everleigh was leaving soon. She was about to disappear for what could be months. *Years.* How could I let her go? How could I let myself lose her all over again?

Ms. Pat was still crying, adding even more to the chaos of

building questions in my mind. "Ms. Pat, calm down and go make coffee. I'm mad, but you have no reason to be crying."

"Actually," Nineteen said, moving closer, "she has a very valid reason to be upset. It's why Eleven and I are here. It's about Alvin."

"What about him?"

My words mirrored Everleigh's. Nineteen paused, then came closer to me. "Eleven and I were in a situation that had us posing as guards. We were approached by two others, the child, his keeper, and...Master Hunt. The Master had convinced the guards he needed to go to his place before returning them to your quarters. After my conversation with the guards, we believe he had ill intentions toward the child. He insisted the guards obey. I intercepted, and without hesitation, took control to bring them home."

"Ill intentions?" Red flashed in my vision and my fists clenched with such strength, they cracked at the force.

"Yes, Main Master. The guards said he and the high leader were whispering before the leader left them with Master Hunt."

Ms. Pat sobbed from the kitchen as words locked in my throat. I turned, stroking down the back of Alvin's head before meeting Everleigh's hard stare.

"Thank you for keeping Alvin safe. I assure you I will deal with this accordingly."

"Of course, Main Master."

Everleigh pulled Alvin closer, swaying with him as his head lowered to rest on her good shoulder. Keeping the rhythm, she made her way closer to Nineteen with watchful eyes. She was reading him.

"You've done good looking after my slave. I'm aware you have a deal with the Main Master concerning this arrangement, but I'd like to show my appreciation as well."

"Mistress, that's not necess—"

"I insist. But with my generosity, there's a price as well. Eleven and I will be leaving here directly. I ask that you please watch over our Main Master as you have looked after my slave. Bram may not like admitting certain things to people, but he is very much in danger. Your loyalty is what he needs more than anything. If you do this, if you stay at his side and protect him until my return, I will match his reward."

"It would be an honor."

"Thank you."

"Wait...*we're leaving*? You're letting me go with you?" Eleven's face lit up, but there was worry there as well. "Where are we going? Can I see my sister?"

"I told you, slave. Layla was payment to Master Draper."

"Actually..." Everleigh's lips pursed in sympathy. She adjusted Alvin on her hip and gave me a guilty look.

"What?" My growl wasn't intentional, but it was threatening at being blindsided by something I didn't know. Eleven rushed up, scanning over Everleigh's face, seeing exactly what I had.

"My sister. Do you have her? Did you rescue her?"

"Not exactly. Let's just say..." Again, she glanced over at me. "Let's just say she's still mine."

"What. The. Hell."

I threw my hands up and headed to the kitchen. I didn't wait for the coffee to finish. I poured myself a cup, cursing Everleigh's pull. She managed to do things I couldn't understand. Why would Master Draper go behind my back and return the slave? Why would he cross me?

"It's Luke," Everleigh rushed out. "I believe he's doing it to gain back his brother's trust or respect. I don't know. All I know is I was told to retrieve her when I was ready." She turned to Eleven. "Do you understand what I'm saying? I need you to focus and let this sink in. You have four options. Only four. You can stay here and continue being a slave. You can delude yourself with fantasies of escape and be rebellious in your attempts, which will land you back in the White Room where death will follow at some point. You can stay. Be a good slave and await my return. Or you can leave with me, try to rebel once we have your sister, which will not only cost you your life, but hers as well. I don't take well to liars. Stop now and let yourself think over those three options. There is no going back, Eleven. If you betray me at any point, just once, you and your twin die. If you don't think you can be found, think again. You know that big medical exam you had when you got here? I'll let you in on a little secret no one but medical personnel and the Main Master know about. Right now, inside you, there is a chip tracking your every move. You won't be able to find it, nor will you have any idea where it is to have it removed. There will not be another me. Whitlock is your home, plain and simple, and you'll never escape it. Ever. So even if I die, they will come for you, and they *will* find you."

Eleven swallowed hard, his shoulders sagging as he wiped away the steady stream of tears.

"Your fourth option, and the one I hope you choose. We leave. You and I will return to Red Island, where we will retrieve your sister, who I hear is being treated like a queen, and the two of you can remain together for the rest of your days. *With me.* You'll be mine. You'll follow my rules, whatever they may be. You'll be loyal, honest, and you'll offer your services. You're a fighter. Will you fight to keep me and Layla safe? Will you verbally accept this contract, and leave with me? If so, you must say it out loud in front of everyone. Tell me you understand what it means to accept it."

A sob tore from his throat as he reached up and buried his fingers in his hair. Slowly, he ran his digits down the tears on his face. Heartbreak, defeat, acceptance—a million things I couldn't begin to read left me staring at a man who was coming to terms with the death of any hope he'd held onto. The only light in all his darkness was his sister which I knew had him nodding.

"I accept, Mistress. I will do whatever you ask me to. I will protect you, obey you. I will never attempt to escape.

"Then we leave. We must go fast." Everleigh was staring down at her phone. She handed Alvin over to me, worry deep in her eyes as she leaned in. "I'm trusting you, taking Eleven with me. If you need to know my whereabouts…track him."

Relief set in at her words. I leaned down, crushing my lips to hers for only a moment. "What's happening?"

"The high leader just left the barracks. He's on his way. Be careful." Everleigh rushed to the room, threw a robe over her shoulders, and stopped as I lifted the hood to fit over the top of her head. My kiss was more desperate. A joining of passion, yet sadness as we broke away from each other. Neither of us said a word as she grabbed Eleven's arm and pulled him to the door. Thin fingers waved to Alvin, and the love of my life disappeared just as fast as she came.

Locking the door at the gesture of my finger, Nineteen headed over, frowning as he let out a deep exhale. "I'm afraid there's more, Main Master."

"More?"

"Yes. A Master. The super archbishop. He's dead."

A groan left me. "You or Eleven?"

"The slave. He witnessed a girl getting thrown out of the apartment. It set him off. I tried to stop him, but…guards came. They didn't know what had happened, but at some point, the Master will be found."

A good minute or two went by as a coverup weaved through my mind. "I'll take care of it. Is that all?"

"Barclane knows I'm still here. He cornered me and the slave. I told him a big story about how I was working with an unnamed source on the Mistress's location. He believes I'm using the slave as bait to lure her out. I forcefully left the situation. I suspect he doesn't believe me."

"Of course he doesn't." I put my hand on Nineteen's shoulder and led him toward the hallway. "I'm aware you made a deal with Everleigh on my safety, but for now, I need you to hide. Go up these stairs," I said, stopping him in front of them, "and do not come down until the high leader leaves. If—"

Banging erupted on the door, causing both our heads to whip over. I pushed Nineteen up the beginning of the stairs and threw him a look as I turned and headed for the door. Loud knocking slammed into the metal, and I gave Ms. Pat a look as she took Alvin and rushed to his bedroom. The moment he was safe, I swung open the barrier. Deep pants were coming from Derek, and he didn't pause as he pushed past me.

"Where is she? I know she was here, and I know her slave came into your quarters as well."

"You're mistaken."

"Bullshit! Did you really think you could reroute my guards off the field and I wouldn't know? She was spotted leaving and no one was there to intercept her. She escaped again, and this time it's on you. Guards!"

Four men eased into the room, trepidation following their every step. Their eyes wouldn't meet mine, but they didn't have to for me to know their intentions. I glared at Derek, seething as he met my stare head-on.

"Bram Whitlock, you are under arrest for harboring and aiding in the escape of fugitives. You will go to the White Room, where you will await sentencing from the board. However long that should take. As of now, Martial Law will go into effect. Whitlock belongs to the guard. *To me.*"

ABOUT THE AUTHOR

A. A. Dark is an International Bestselling Author. She doesn't reside in one place for long and is known to move at the drop of a dime. From mountains and snow to tropical beaches, she could be at one in the morning and the other by night. A. A. is a Goodread's 2016 Choice Award Finalist in Horror. She is also the CEO of Mad Girl Publishing and the founder for the Pitch Black brand.

CAUTION when reading.

Newsletter:　　　http://alaskaangelini.us9.list-manage1.com/subscribe?u=bab41358f98da39a35c46dccb&id=19172fa88c

Get the last installment of the 24690 series now!